"In the Abigail books, Bethany captures a loving family's commitment to their faith as their nine-year-old girl navigates the everyday challenges of life. This book not only tells a clever, funny story about Abigail but also successfully unpacks the biblical truths that Abigail discovers along the way."

Bob Hartman, Author and Storyteller

"Starting over is hard! But it's a lesson nine-year-old Abigail is learning as she begins fourth grade at her new school. She's also going to learn about grace—the kind we extend to others and the grace God offers his children. Fun, relatable, grounded in Scripture, and full of bold illustrations, *Abigail and the Big Start Over* by Bethany McIlrath is a story kids will love."

Amanda Cleary Eastep, Author, Tree Street Kids series

"Bethany has created a delightful series that helps young readers connect their faith with their everyday life. Abigail's adventures are fun and relatable, delivering valuable lessons for all kids and making this series a great one to add to your bookshelf."

Laura Wifler, Cofounder, Risen Motherhood

"While plenty of books for kids this age have 'good guys' and 'bad guys,' Bethany McIlrath has crafted real-world characters in real-life settings who exhibit both vice and virtue and desperately need God's grace for a fresh start. Honestly, that was my favorite trait of this book—how all the characters demonstrate their need for grace, from Abigail to her new friend Flora, to their irritating classmate Greg, to Abigail's mom. This engaging book will help kids honor others, seek to understand others, extend grace to others, and grow in grace themselves."

Caroline Saunders, Author, *Remarkable: The Gospel of Mark*

"Bethany McIlrath has written a fabulous book that somehow entertains while it teaches truth!"

Dannah Gresh, Author, *Lies Girls Believe and the Truth That Sets Them Free*

"Delightful. Relatable. Entertaining. Accessible. True. Meeting Abigail in these pages felt like discovering a friend for the fifth-grade 'new girl' inside of me, who was desperately lonely and felt like she was blowing it at every turn. I am so eager to introduce *Abigail and the Big Start Over* to all of my elementary-aged friends so that they too can adventure with her, identify with her, and discover the incredibly beautiful and immensely applicable power of the gospel in their own very real lives, right alongside her. These stories about Abigail will doubtless impact the stories of their readers in a powerful way."

Abbey Wedgeworth, Author, Training Young Hearts series

"I love the way Bethany McIlrath shapes her books! It really feels like you're there with the characters."

Nora, age 12

"I like how Abigail thinks about the Bible and Jesus."

Zion, age 8

"*Abigail and the Big Start Over* shows that all girls need a friend. I think this will show readers that they're never alone and God is with them."

Adelaide, age 9

"Abigail's story is a lot like mine: moving, new school friends, and using my imagination."

Judah, age 10

Abigail and the BIG Start Over

Written by
Bethany McIlrath

Illustrated by
Katie Saunders

Abigail and the Big Start Over
© Bethany McIlrath, 2024.

Published by:
The Good Book Company

thegoodbook.com | thegoodbook.co.uk
thegoodbook.com.au | thegoodbook.co.nz | thegoodbook.co.in

Unless indicated, all Scripture references are taken from the Holy Bible, New International Reader's Version®, NIrV®. Copyright © 2014 Biblica, Inc.™ Used by permission of Zondervan.

All rights reserved. Except as may be permitted by the Copyright Act, no part of this publication may be reproduced in any form or by any means without prior permission from the publisher.

Bethany McIlrath has asserted her right under the Copyright, Designs and Patents Act 1988 to be identified as author of this work.

Illustrated by Katie Saunders | Design and Art Direction by André Parker

ISBN: 9781784988982 | Printed in Turkey

Contents

1. Hurry Up, Headband — 7
2. Mrs. Hennig — 15
3. Don't Forget the Fishing Pole — 23
4. Brown, Slimy Sludge — 31
5. Uh Oh! — 39
6. Flora Flores — 47
7. Big Mouths — 57
8. A Very Good Friend — 63
9. Kids' Club — 71
10. Peter's Big Adventure — 81
11. Fisher of Men — 89
12. Nana and Grandpa's — 97
13. Sticky-Duct-Aids — 105
14. Walking on Water — 115
15. Greg Again — 125

16. We Need to Talk	133
17. Adventure Central	141
18. A Good Grace Story	149
19. Fantastic Flora	159
20. Not Such a Mess	165
21. Adventuring	173
22. Second Chances	181
A Note from the Author	189
A Sneak Peek	193
Book-Club Questions	199
Acknowledgments	205

Chapter One
Hurry Up, Headband

New, new, new!

Abigail sang happily in her head as she sat down on the front seat of the bus, straightened the pretty, new headband she was wearing, and got ready to smile. *Please God,* she thought, *let the next kid who steps onto the bus be someone super fun!*

She pulled her carefully decorated, new pencil case out of her backpack, slipping it onto the seat next to her. Its purple polka dots sparkled and glittered. In her mind, she played out the conversation she'd have with the kid who sat next to her on the bus. It was going to go just as she'd imagined it every single day while she was staying at her cousin's for the summer.

"Your glitter pencil case is awesome," the kid would say.

"Oh thanks, I got it when I turned nine in May," Abigail would say back in her coolest fourth-grader voice. "But it's not a pencil case."

"It's not?" they'd ask, sitting down next to her, super-curious.

"It's my Amazing Adventure Box!" Abigail was all ready to answer. Then she'd whip it open, flashing her rainbow sticky-note stack and pulling out the chunky multi-pen she could pick any color from. She'd

ask her new friend a surprising question like "Where's the most awesome place you've ever been?" And they would say someplace like Australia or, even better, the moon! She'd pop down their favorite color on her multi-pen and start doodling and writing and sticking up the notes on the window. Before you knew it, all the kids on the bus would move to sit nearby, and they'd spend the whole journey imagining adventures together! And even better, Abigail would be able to invite her new friends over to her new house, where Mom had promised they'd make a new "Adventure Central" space in her new room.

That was how this new year at this new school was going to start. Abigail just knew it.

WHOOSH! The door opened as the bus came to a stop. Abigail smiled eagerly as she waited to meet her new friend.

But…

"Move it, headband!"

A boy had reached the top of the dusty school-bus steps. He had dark hair and red sneakers, and he was staring right at Abigail.

"Move it, headband!" he said again.

Abigail reached up to touch the pretty new headband she was wearing. "Do you... do you mean me?"

"Yeah," the boy grunted, shuffling his sneakers impatiently. "This is my seat. You don't belong here."

Suddenly the purple polka dots on Abigail's Amazing Adventure Box didn't seem quite so sparkly. She wished she could disappear.

"Oh," she said in a tiny voice, grabbing her things as someone from the back of the bus yelled, "Hey, Greg!"

"Hey," the mean boy said grumpily, not moving his eyes from Abigail. "Hurry up, headband."

Abigail stood up to find another slippy brown seat, nervously scanning all the unfamiliar faces staring at her. They'd all heard what mean Greg had said. She wondered if everyone at her new school was always going to call her "headband" now.

"No standing!" the school-bus driver exclaimed over a loudspeaker.

Abigail chose a seat and dropped down into it as fast as she could.

THUMP. Her headband slumped off onto the empty seat next to her. She felt like throwing it.

That morning the headband had seemed like the best part of her new school outfit. It was extra big and glittery, and it had all her favorite colors in its stripes: yellow, orange, blue, purple. Plus, Mom had said the rubbery part inside would hold it in place. *So much for that*, Abigail thought. *I love these things, but they NEVER stay!*

It wasn't just the headband either. Abigail suddenly remembered how worried she was that everything was slipping right out of place. Her new house was bigger than the old one across town, but it didn't feel like home. She'd been excited to make friends fast at her new school, but now that she was on the bus, all alone, hearing all the other kids chattering without her, she wasn't so sure.

Dad called all the changes "the Big Start Over," like they were on some big adventure. That would be awesome. Abigail loved adventures! But she wondered if her mom was right. "The Big Mess." That was what Mom called it.

Her parents did agree on one thing: they were all going to need grace to get them through so much change. Abigail wasn't sure what grace was, but she figured she needed a lot of it.

Feeling the bus come to another stop, she looked out of the window and saw a big gray cinderblock building. Above the door was a big gray sign which said Corolla Elementary.

GULP. There wasn't going to be any adventure here—just boredom and loneliness! Abigail wished she was back in her old room, in her old house, getting ready to go to her old school with all the friends she already had. *New, new, new,* she thought, but this time the words sounded scary instead of exciting.

Climbing down from the bus, Abigail followed the crowd toward the school.

At least my teacher might be nice, she thought. *And please God, don't let Greg be in my class!*

Chapter Two

Mrs. Hennig

Abigail walked into the fourth-grade classroom, reaching up to slide her multicolored headband back into place yet again. She chose an empty desk and glanced around at the unfamiliar red seats and the faces she didn't know. She hoped somebody would talk to her.

"Are you Miss Abigail Brenner?" asked a tall, thin lady with her hands on her hips. Her slicked-back red hair and pointy glasses made her look like a cartoon character—the kind Abigail and her friends used to draw as the

bad guy for their stories and imaginary adventures. *Not* the sort of person Abigail had been hoping would talk to her.

"Yes?" Abigail answered, wishing she was anybody else, anywhere else.

"Welcome," the lady said in a raspy voice that didn't sound very welcoming. She handed Abigail some papers.

"You and your parents should have those forms filled in by tomorrow at the latest, please," she said.

Then, without another word, she turned away and walked up to another girl—one with curly, dark hair and a huge flower headband. The lady was handing this girl some papers too—but Abigail barely had time to notice. She was too busy begging God in her mind: *Please, please let this stiff lady not be my teacher!*

WHEEE!

Now the lady with the slick red hair was standing at the front of the classroom, blowing a shiny silver whistle.

"Hello class," she said flatly as everyone found a seat and fell silent. "I'm your teacher, Mrs. Hennig."

Abigail gulped.

Mrs. Hennig held up the whistle and peered at them all through her pointy glasses. "I should never have to use this again, right? This year will be good for all of us if I don't need my whistle. I don't like to have to speak loudly."

Abigail nodded along with everyone else, wondering when the ringing in her ears would stop.

"Welcome to fourth grade," Mrs. Hennig continued, folding her hands in front of her like she was praying. "I expect you to behave like ladies and gentlemen."

SNORT!

Looking at the seat next to her, Abigail instantly recognized the kid who'd made the noise.

Greg.

Oh no. Abigail looked away quickly, staring ahead at her teacher. Maybe Mrs. Hennig would smile, or grin, or even pull her mouth into a straight line instead of a scowl. But it didn't seem possible!

Is her face stuck like that? Abigail wondered, squinting.

Then she smiled. That would make for a great game! She could have a face-holding contest with her friends... when she had friends here, anyway. She would have to remember to write that idea down on her rainbow sticky notes.

"Every day when the bell rings," Mrs. Hennig said, "you take out your math workbooks and begin one practice lesson."

RINNNGGG!

Abigail jumped, banging her knee on her desk. Great, now she'd get a bruise. She tried not to make a noise while she fumbled with all the books on the shelf under her desk to find the one about math.

I didn't miss math over the summer, she sighed inwardly as she heaved the thick workbook onto her desk. The first problem looked hard. She counted on her fingers under the desk, just in case that was cheating in fourth-grade math. Give Abigail a random word or picture and she could come up with all sorts of fun ideas and stories and games—but numbers? **BLEH!**

"Ahem," Mrs. Hennig suddenly coughed, standing tall at the front of the room again. "Miss Brenner."

Mrs. Hennig was staring right at Abigail. Abigail cringed—she'd been caught counting on her fingers! She braced herself for the whole class to hear about it. Now she was going to be the girl who couldn't keep a headband on to save her life and couldn't do math!

But all Mrs. Hennig said was "Please tell us your answer for the first question."

Please let this be right, God, Abigail prayed in her mind as she squeaked out, "Umm... 9?"

Shaking her head no, Mrs. Hennig ran a hand over her slick red hair as she called on someone else.

Abigail blushed bright red as she scrunched down in her seat and caught her headband as it slipped off. Again. Yup, she was officially Abigail, the can't-do-math-can't-keep-a-headband-on-fourth-grade-failure.

Staring at the sandals on her feet, Abigail thought how she'd rather be dipping her toes in the pool back at her cousin Gracie's house. Back before they moved, and everything changed.

New Student Information

Name: Abigail Brenner

Date of birth: 26th May

Address: 44 Avonlea Lane

Parents' names:

Hank Brenner

Susanna Brenner

Health issues:

Allergy to Caterpillars

Favorite subject:

Art / Reading

Least favorite subject:

Math

⭐ Chapter Three

Don't Forget the Fishing Pole

Mrs. Hennig wrote out more math problems on the board, but it was hard to concentrate. By halfway through the lesson, Abigail was slumped over her workbook, doodling in the edges as she remembered how her cousin Gracie had taught her how to do dolphin flips in the pool and how to whistle.

She sketched a wavy line for water and a little dolphin popping up out of it. She loved how magical they looked! So much better than fish.

Abigail sighed. The thought of fish reminded her of the Bible story Mom never finished telling her that weekend about a guy called

Simon at the sea. Mom said Simon was also called Peter. Did Simon Peter ever see dolphins?

Gracie would know, Abigail thought. Gracie was a fifth grader, and she'd already memorized 217 Bible verses. That was what she said, anyway.

Normally, Abigail liked Bible time with her family, but Mom had rushed right through the cool new orange book their church had given them to read alongside the Bible. "We just have to get it done!" she had kept muttering. Church kids' club was going to start later that week, and Abigail guessed Mom was worried all the other kids would know the story and Abigail wouldn't.

The Bible story had started off good. Peter and his friends were in a boat, so it sounded like an adventure! And friendship adventure stories were awesome. Abigail had just started imagining the sunshine and the sound of the waves when Mom had skipped right to the part of the story with… **GULP.** Fishing.

Abigail imagined how slippery and scaly fish would feel and how stinky it must have been.

How can anybody swim where fish go to the bathroom?! she wondered as she kept drawing her magical-looking dolphins.

"Psst," Greg hissed across the aisle. "Psst. You forgot the fishing pole!"

Abigail ignored him. *Can't he see this is a dolphin?* she thought. *Besides, fishing is gross!* In the story Mom told, Abigail figured that when Jesus showed up, he'd get rid of the stinky fish and send the friends off to do something good, since Jesus was always doing good things, but no! He actually told them to go fish again!

She crinkled up her nose just thinking about fish and their smelliness. Then she sighed. The problem with the story wasn't just the stinky fish. Mom had skipped all the questions in the book from church too, so Abigail hadn't even had a turn to say anything! What if at kids' club everyone else already knew all the answers? Her church friends would think she was bad at Bible stuff, just like all the kids in her new class probably thought she was bad at math and headbands!

Abigail tightened her grip on her pencil, smooshing the lines for the waves together like the water was wild.

"Psst!" Greg said again. He started fiddling with his pencil case. It had black birds with big yellow beaks all over it, but it wasn't glittery like Abigail's Adventure Box. Abigail looked back at her box with a smile. Then she almost yelped as Greg reached across with a pencil like he was going to fix her picture. "Your drawing is missing stuff. Come on, let me..."

Abigail scooched a little farther away in her desk, twisting herself and her workbook doodles away. *I just have to keep ignoring him,* she thought. But Greg got louder.

"Hey," he exclaimed, "the line! Don't forget the fishing line!"

"Excuse me," came a stern voice from the front of the classroom. Mrs. Hennig was straightening her pointy glasses as she came toward them. "Do you have a question?"

Abigail tried to hide her doodles.

"No," Greg mumbled. "No problem."

"Please pay attention to your own work," Mrs. Hennig snapped, shaking her fiery-red hair as she moved to the front of the room again.

Greg sighed loudly and muttered something else about fishing.

Abigail bit her lip. She'd escaped being told off... for now.

Chapter Four

Brown, Slimy Sludge

By the time Abigail got on the bus again, her stomach ached. Her hair was a mess from fixing her headband all day, she was really nervous about how strict Mrs. Hennig was, and she'd never even had a chance to open her Amazing Adventure Box so she hadn't even got to try to make new friends.

All by herself on the bus, listening to the other kids talking, Abigail sketched H-O-M-E in tiny bubble letters and green ink on a sticky note from her glittery box. The green was because that was the color of her old home. This new house was just plain old brown. What a terrible color. Her multi-pen didn't even have brown in it.

Abigail tried to cheer up by daydreaming about the new Adventure Central which Mom had promised.

"In your new room," Mom had said, "we're going to have an awesome space where you can stick your notes, and decorate, and dream, and plan all your coolest, craziest games and stories with your friends!" And it was going to be ready just in time for Abigail to celebrate starting at her new school. That meant today!

She wasn't sure what her new Adventure Central would be like exactly, but that wasn't going to stop Abigail dreaming. She imagined a ginormous bulletin board and glittery pushpins and shiny papers cut by her crazy-edge scissors. She was going to hang up the picture of herself and her friends at her church's kids' club. At least she hadn't moved to a different church as well as house and school.

Right next to the picture of her church friends, she'd keep track of all the stuff she wanted to win too. Like the fourth-grade story-writing contest in town. And a sticker every week at Sunday school for memorizing the Bible verse.

My first verse is... umm. Abigail tried to remember it. *Grow in the grace... and something... of Jesus? Peter 3?* It was definitely something to do with Peter, the man from the icky fish story.

But it didn't matter that she couldn't remember the memory verse exactly yet. Soon she'd be writing it in... ADVENTURE CENTRAL! Abigail smiled, feeling cheered up again. Probably getting Adventure Central ready was why Mom had been so busy, she realized. Maybe Adventure Central was more work for Mom than a bulletin board... Maybe it was a special fort, or a mega desk, or...

"Brenner, Abigail Brenner," the bus driver shouted as he stopped. Looking out of the window, Abigail remembered that the house she lived in now was not fun or bright like she preferred. It wasn't like her old home back on Hickory Avenue, where dandelions grew in the squiggly cracks in the driveway and Mom's flowers were so colorful the yard felt like a party. This house had no flowers, no cool cracks in the driveway, and hardly any color at all.

Abigail slinked off the bus quietly, hoping Greg wouldn't notice her and yell about her headband or crazy hair or whatever else he might pick on.

It's going to be okay, she told herself, trying not to notice the tall, plain brown walls or stark, flowerless yard as she reached the front door. Hopefully her Adventure Central would have colors—maybe even yellow, orange, blue and purple!

She turned the knob on the front door and walked in.

But her mom wasn't there waiting with first-day snacks or hugs or anything. Not even her baby brother Henry was there, exclaiming her name in his toddler talk. "Gabigaa!" he loved to say. Sometimes it annoyed her that he couldn't say it right, but today she'd give anything to be called something other than "headband"!

Catching that exact headband as it slipped off yet again, Abigail dropped her backpack by the door and trudged toward her room.

Wishing she could go back to her old house and her old life as her stomach growled for after-school snacks, she also wished Mom would stop being so busy getting the new house ready. She shuddered slightly, hoping this Adventure Central would be worth it.

Abigail passed a pile of broken-down boxes leaning against the wall in the hall where her dad had left them after they'd unpacked her stuff the night before. The pile was bigger than before... but none of the newly broken boxes said Adventure Central on them.

There is no way Mom forgot, Abigail told herself confidently. She'd promised.

CREEEAK. Abigail squeezed her eyes shut as she pushed open the door, her stomach a jumble of fear and excitement.

"Uh oh!" exclaimed Henry.

Abigail's eyes shot open.

There was Henry, in the middle of Abigail's bedroom, covered in brown, slimy sludge. He looked around wildly as Abigail glanced around too.

No awesome Adventure Central in sight. Not even a plain old bulletin board. No cool new poster even. All the stuff she and her dad had set up so her room wouldn't feel so weird was covered in plastic. And the plastic was covered in... brown stuff.

"Henry!" Abigail whispered as her stomach groaned. "What did you do?"

"Uh oh," Henry said again, his voice louder.

Like big sisters know they sometimes have to do, Abigail took a deep breath and a big sniff. Because sometimes, when baby brothers are covered in brown stuff, it's...

WHEW. This was no toilet issue. But what was it?

Tip-toeing her way across the crunchy plastic that was everywhere, Abigail found the biggest brown puddle of all. It was on the floor—right in the middle of four tipped-over paint cans.

Chapter Five

Uh Oh!

"Henry?" Mom's voice called out. "Where are you? The bus will be here any minute! We need to get ready for Abby to come home to her surprise!"

Abigail looked from the puddle of paint to her slimy little brother. Some surprise!

"Henry?" Mom called again.

"Uh oh," Henry repeated, taking off at a run as fast as he could. His bare, brown, wet feet pattered across the crunchy plastic right out onto the hallway carpet and toward the kitchen.

"Uh oh, uh oh," Henry yelled, leaving a trail of gooey brown paint behind him as he kept on running.

Abigail just stood there, staring down. It looked like the paint used to be blue, purple, yellow, and orange—all her favorite colors. That was what the little bit left in each can was, anyway. Now it was mostly brown. Puddled on the plastic on the floor. Splattered around on the plastic on the furniture. And... Abigail squinted. Yup. Splashed onto the plastic over her bed.

Where was her adventure space? What was the paint for? Abigail tried to make sense of it. What about the awesome stories, and the spots for sticky notes and crazy games, and all the things that would make this room feel like home? And all the best colors were the worst color now!

Hearing Mom call after Henry again, Abigail

found herself repeating in a whisper, "But Mom promised. She promised!"

Her shoulders shook. Her stomach ached. And her headband...

PLOP.

Right off her head. Right into the puddle of paint.

Abigail's face got wet, but not from the puddle. She stumbled toward her bed, looking for a tissue or her favorite stuffed red panda, Pedro, or anything that might make it all okay. But her tears were so fast and so many, she could hardly see. Her feet started to slip...

WHAM!

Abigail hit the floor. Sitting up painfully, she tried to swipe the tears from her eyes. She looked down at herself. Now it wasn't just her headband that was brown—so were her school clothes. Her *new* school clothes.

"Abby?"

Mom was suddenly standing in the brown-splattered doorway with a squirming, splattered brown Henry in her arms.

Abigail's lip shook as the tears kept falling, falling, falling. Her nose was getting all runny and warm. She wasn't even worried about making a mess. How could anything be messier than it already was?

"What happened?" Mom said. "When did you get home?"

"Henry," Abigail tried to say, but she couldn't get any more words to come out making sense.

"Your school clothes... your headband..." Mom reached out a hand to help Abigail up. "Oh, Henry Abraham and Abigail Ruth!"

"But..." Abigail tried again to speak, but she stopped when she tasted more than salty tears on her face. Was that... paint... on her face... in her mouth!? "Ick, ick, ick!" she exclaimed.

"Ick is right!" Mom said, tapping her foot like she was going to lose it. "Bathroom. Right now. I can't believe this."

After that Mom just kept talking, not to anyone really, just talking and talking in a grumpy way.

"It was supposed to be a nice surprise," she said as she got Henry all cleaned up.

"I don't have time for this," she muttered when it was Abigail's turn.

"Ruined. Ruined. Ruined," she sighed as she stuck Henry's play clothes and Abigail's school clothes in the washing machine.

I just don't understand, Abigail thought as she sat on the couch with Henry, watching his little toddler shows. Mom had never been like this before. Abigail didn't like anything about this Big Start Over Mess!

"Gabigaa..." Henry said, scooting close until his soft, puffy toddler arms were right up against hers. "Gabigaa?"

"Hmm?" Abigail said, looking down at her baby brother.

"Bett-ah?" he asked, mumbling a few other toddler words she couldn't make out. "Gabigaa bett-ah?"

"Better?" Abigail repeated, sighing. She looked at his little red face, big eyes looking hopefully into hers. "From the big mess you made?

He looked away, very sorry.

"Yeah," Abigail said, taking a deep breath and trying not to sound as mad and sad as she'd been feeling. "Yes, Abigail better." Whatever

Henry messed up, she still loved him.

Henry hopped out of the room and made a little noise in the hallway. When he came back, he was holding something glittery. Something rectangular. The Amazing Adventure Box! Abigail grinned. It was no Adventure Central, but it was enough to cheer her up.

"Want to invent something awesome together?" she asked Henry, grinning as she wiggled her eyebrows up and down.

Based on Henry's clapping, it was a yes!

Chapter Six

Flora Flores

Well, I'm a friendless fourth-grade failure, Abigail groaned to herself as she got off the bus and walked through the faded red doors of Corolla Elementary. She'd dug and dug through her backpack, and the paper from Mrs. Hennig wasn't there. She knew Dad had filled it out before he'd tucked her in on the couch last night. But now she didn't have it!

Walking toward her classroom nervously, Abigail wondered what happens to friendless fourth-grade failures. In one movie she'd seen, bad kids got locked in a dark, smelly closet with nails poking out all over, but their friends rescued them. Abigail didn't have anyone to help defend her from Mrs. Hennig. The only person she knew was Greg, and he sure wouldn't!

Abigail sighed as her mind drifted back to the story about Peter and Jesus. They were like best friends, Mom had said. Peter even let

Jesus ride in his boat, and Jesus healed people, and Peter got to watch.

I bet if I had a boat or I could heal people and do miracles and stuff, I would have friends, Abigail thought as she looked around the hallway at all the faces she didn't know, latching her eyes onto a girl with her arm in a sling and smiling. **POOF!** *I could fix that girl's arm! Then she'd be my bestie!*

"What are you staring at?" the girl snapped, rolling her eyes as she turned her back to talk to some other kids.

Abigail blushed, feeling like everyone was staring at her yet again.

Sometimes people don't start off well, she told herself, *but they end up being best friends anyway.* Even Peter and Jesus had had some problems in their friendship, Mom had said. Peter had messed up somehow—Mom hadn't explained how—but Jesus had forgiven him.

So maybe the girl with the sling would end up being her bestie. That would be funny, right?

"Hey! Abigail?" said a voice suddenly. A smiley girl popped up beside her. "That's your name, right?"

"Hi," Abigail said back hesitantly. Slowly she recognized the thick dark curls and tan face of the other new girl who got a paper from Mrs. Hennig yesterday. The one with the floral headband—although today the girl just had one huge fake flower pinned on her head. It was fluffy and pink and even bigger than the wide smile on her face.

Here we go, Abigail thought. *I hope I don't mess this up like Peter did! Whatever it was he did...* She wished she knew so that she wouldn't do the same thing as him.

"I'm Flora Flores," the energetic girl offered, spreading her hands like she was announcing herself on a stage. She was definitely dressed like she could be on stage! She wore neon shorts and a shirt with the biggest, most purple flower on it.

Before Abigail even had time to think, Flora went on. "I heard Mrs. Hennig say in class you're new. I'm new too. Being new is weird, right? I don't know anyone here. But I guess I'll make friends fast. Fun, fantastic friends. Do you have any friends yet? Where did you move from?"

"Ummm," Abigail answered, trying to figure out which question to answer first.

Laughing, Flora slapped her on the back, "Hey, it's okay, chica. Chica means "girl" in Spanish. Can I call you that? I love nicknames. Don't you love nicknames? If I could pick a new name, I would ask everyone to call me Flora the Fantastical Flower Fairy. That's a long nickname. But guess what? It has alliteration. That's when words all start with the same letter, and it sounds awesome. Do you already have a nickname?"

This chica talks more than I do! And that's a lot! Abigail thought, fumbling for words to respond. "You can call me Chica," she mustered, looking at the chatty, confident girl very curiously. Flora's Big Start Over didn't seem like such a big mess...

"Did you and your parents have to do that new-kid paper for Mrs. Hennig already, Chica?" Flora asked.

Abigail knew the answer to that one! Before Flora could pour out a whole flood of words again, Abigail said, "Yeah, but... I forgot mine. Well, I did it. My dad did it. But we just moved, and things are crazy and..."

Pausing for a sudden high-five, Flora announced, "I forgot too. I guess we'll be the first fantastic fourth-grade failure friends together! Do you get it? Alliteration! And F is the grade of failures!"

She giggled so hard Abigail couldn't help joining in. Something about Flora's silliness was contagious!

"We can stick together if we get in trouble about the paper!" Abigail said, forgetting her nerves and her fears as she laughed.

"Yes!" Flora practically shouted with a huge smile. "And guess what? There's this cool park near my house my mom says I can explore on Friday after school with a new friend! Want to come? Ask your mom!"

"Yes!" Abigail exclaimed, already feeling her hands tingle at the thought of climbing some big rocks with a friend and having a real-life adventure to match her imaginary ones. "I love being outside! And adventures! What do you like doing at the park? This one time I..."

"Sorry, Chica-friend," Flora interrupted happily as they entered the classroom and parted for their desks, "Let's sit together at lunch today! We can talk the WHOLE time!"

Grinning to herself, Abigail took a deep breath as she sank into her seat and tried not to look at mean Greg next to her, or at Mrs. Hennig pacing the front of the room with her whistle.

I just have to make it to lunch, she thought. Then—friend time! She quickly jotted down some alliteration on her sticky notes. Alliteration was kind of like a game. Abigail hoped Flora liked games and adventures as much as she did!

Chapter Seven

Big Mouths

RINNNGGG!

Flora slipped right behind Abigail in line for lunch, flouncing her curls and smiling wider than anyone Abigail had ever known.

"Hey, Chica! Yay, we're in lunch together!" Flora said as soon as they got to the table. "Guess what? I know the end of the story we're reading in class! It's the best! You'd never believe it! Want to hear it?"

"Wait," Abigail exclaimed as she unzipped her lunch bag. "No spoilers! I want to see if I guessed the ending right. It's like a game."

"Okaaay," Flora giggled, making the word sound a little like the start of a song. "Where's your headband, by the way? I loved it yesterday! I didn't get to tell you. Purple and blue are my favorite colors. It had lots of purple and blue!"

"Purple and blue are two of my four favorites too!" Abigail exclaimed. But then her face fell. "My headband got ruined though..."

"Oh no," Flora said, taking a big bite of her sandwich. "What happened?"

"Well..." Abigail answered, and then it all spilled out. How they'd moved, how her mom had been so stressed out, how Abigail had come home to a big mess her brother had made in her room—and she'd got blamed for it!

"That's not fair," Flora said.

Abigail nodded, sighing. "I know, right?" She felt even better after talking about it. Flora sure could talk a lot, but she was also a good listener, and she didn't seem to mind Abigail talking a lot too—at least when she was eating! "My dad would probably say something about grace or another Bible thing, but I don't really…"

"Hey!" a familiar voice interrupted.

"Uh oh," Abigail muttered under her breath.

"Hey!" Greg said again. "You're the new kids, right?"

"Yeah," Flora replied, "Your name's Greg, isn't it? I saw you had toucans on your pencil case. The black birds with the yellow beaks, right? My Nana is from Ecuador, and there are lots of toucans there. I visited this summer. Have you ever seen a toucan in real life? They have really big mouths!"

"Talk about big mouths," Greg smirked back, "what're your names?"

Before Abigail could answer, Flora kept going.

Didn't she notice his insult about her big mouth? Abigail wondered. *It was so rude!*

"I'm Flora," Flora explained, spreading her hands like she was on stage, just like she had that morning. "And you are...?"

Greg just laughed. "Your name is *Floor*?"

"No," Flora answered, her voice suddenly quiet.

"Hey, everybody!" Greg shouted to the rest of the table as all the faces Abigail and Flora didn't even know yet turned their way. "Her name is FLOOR. Like dirty, sticky, muddy, gross floors! Isn't that funny?!"

Looking at her new friend, Abigail saw the bubbly, silly chica grow weirdly quiet. Flora's bright eyes weren't shining anymore—they were staring all dark and sad at the brown-tile cafeteria floor.

"Ew!" another boy exclaimed.

"That's a terrible name," one blonde-haired girl commented. "The floor is filthy. Just look at it!"

Greg just laughed and laughed.

Abigail felt like the half-sandwich in her belly weighed a ton, and like the jelly in it must have been spicy because her cheeks burned red hot. She marched right off to tell a grown-up about Greg being a bully. This was NOT okay!

Mrs. Hennig just heard Greg's name and the word "bully" and called him over before Abigail could explain in detail. With a hand on her hip, she asked Greg and Abigail, "Now, what's the problem?"

"Beats me," Greg shrugged, jerking his thumb at Abigail. "I didn't do anything to her!"

"That's not true!" Abigail protested. "Well, not exactly," she tried to explain. Greg hadn't bullied *her*.

"Miss Brenner," Mrs. Hennig said, tapping her foot on the floor impatiently, "you said Greg was being a bully. Was that true, or wasn't it?"

"No," snapped Greg, "she cried wolf! I didn't bully her! I don't even know her name!"

"But Greg did say a mean name!" Abigail said, her face turning red as Greg rolled his eyes at her.

"Liar, liar, wolf pants on fire!" Greg mocked.

"Enough!" Mrs. Hennig said.

With a little shudder, Abigail glanced back at the table. Flora's pretty dark curls were mashed up on the table where she'd laid her head down and was sitting all lonely and silent still.

This just wasn't okay!

Chapter Eight

A Very Good Friend

"If we can't sort this out in the next minute," Mrs. Hennig said, both hands on her hips, "I'm going to have to call your parents."

I didn't do anything wrong! Abigail shouted inside. Then, getting real quiet in her head, she asked God to help her. What else could she do?

Greg looked at Abigail and quietly howled again, putting his hands on his hips too.

"But Mrs. Hennig!" Abigail exclaimed, trying to get it all out at once, "Greg called Flora dirty floors and got everybody to laugh at her! He is being a bully! Not to me—to Flora! He made fun of her name! He said she is gross and muddy, like the floors!"

Greg's face turned bright red as Mrs. Hennig's nostrils began to flare.

"I was trying to be funny," he said.

Mrs. Hennig stood up straight, dropping her arms to her sides. "Miss Abigail Brenner," she said in a voice that was surprisingly nice, "thank you for telling me what happened. You go back to your friend Flora."

Greg did not get to go back to the table. He and Mrs. Hennig were gone by the time Abigail slid in next to Flora again.

"Hey, Chica," Abigail said, touching Flora's shoulder gently. "I told Mrs. Hennig. Greg is getting in trouble."

"Thanks," Flora said, raising her head and quickly wiping her nose like she'd been crying. "You're a good friend."

Abigail's heart smiled big. She hadn't messed up like Peter! She'd done the right thing! Now Flora was her friend forever.

"So," she said, trying to cheer Flora up, "I've never seen a toucan or a real-life bird. No," she giggled, "I've seen birds. But not like a pet bird. Except in a movie! Do birds like to be pet? My Nana and Grandpa have a cat called Snickers. She looooves to be pet!"

Flora's loud, silly laugh rang out so strongly some kids looked at her.

"Toucans aren't pets!" she smiled. "They're wild birds—we always see them when we visit Ecuador. Like umm... pigeons! Kind of. Anyway, guess what? They have beaks this long!"

Flora stretched her hands out even bigger than her sandwich. "Their beaks are as big as their whole bodies, and they're not just yellow actually. Some of them have different bright, fun colors like... like... flowers or rainbows or unicorns! And guess what? They hop! I mean, they fly too, but they like to hop-hop-hop around." She bounced in her seat as she explained. Abigail noticed that lots of other kids had started listening too.

"What colors?" she asked, pulling her Amazing Adventure Box out from under her lunch bag. She popped it open and held up her nifty multi-pen.

"What do you keep in that shiny box?" a sandy-haired boy asked curiously.

"Well, it's my magical multi-pen," Abigail explained, quickly popping the blue color button down and scribbling, then switching to green, then to purple. "See? It lets me switch between colors super fast like this!"

"Can I try?" a soft-spoken girl asked. As the

girl scribbled on a sticky note, changing colors as wildly and quickly as she could, Flora talked about other birds she knew about.

"You know a lot about birds," the sandy-haired boy said. "Maybe you should be a scientist. I saw a documentary once where people went into the jungle and recorded bird calls and things. They could tell what the bird was just by listening."

Flora grinned. "Maybe I will. Adventures in the jungle! The joyous, jaunty, joking, juh… juh… jagged jungle!" She paused. "Me and Abigail are adventurer buddies."

"Yeah," Abigail added, feeling her heart swell. "We're even going on a big adventure

on Friday! Like a real-life one—not just imaginary!"

"Is this where you keep imaginary adventures?" the girl with the quiet voice asked shyly as she handed back the multi-pen and peeked under the glittery lid of Abigail's box.

"Yeah!" Abigail answered excitedly, pulling out her best grin and eyebrow wiggle. "Want to have one right now?"

"You go, Chica!" Flora clapped.

"Okay," Abigail said, leaning in and letting her brain run wild... wild like... an animal! Like a toucan, maybe! "Here! Everybody tell me the craziest animal you ever saw!"

She jotted each one down on its own sticky note in the color that matched the animal the best. Then she and Flora and five whole other kids put them out two at a time and voted on who would win things like "coolest looking" or "smelliest" or "best pet."

"You're really good at making friends," Abigail whispered to Flora as they got back in line for class, barely noticing as a red-faced Greg slipped into the back, far away from them.

"You're very good at *being* a friend, Chica," Flora said, spreading her hands out just like she did when she said her name.

That feels very official! Abigail smiled to herself. *Miss Abigail Chica Brenner, "The very good friend!"* *Thank you, God!*

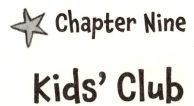
Chapter Nine
Kids' Club

Miss Abigail Chica Brenner did not have an Adventure Central in her room when she got home. In fact, a piece of boring, ugly cardboard, taller than her, blocked the door.

"Sorry, Abby," Mom said, rushing by with a squirming Henry on her hip. "I didn't have time today, and tonight is church stuff."

I still don't get to be in my room? Abigail moaned inside. *How long do I have to wait for this Adventure Central?*

But she couldn't be too sad. She had at least

one friend at school, and "church stuff" meant kids' club. She had lots of friends there. They'd been playing games and learning about God and the Bible and singing songs every week for... well, as long as she could remember!

Of course, she would be in fourth-grade kids' club now. Same kids but a different leader. They'd probably do all the same stuff though. They'd *definitely* do memory verses.

"Grow in grace and... something... something..." Abigail tried to remember the verse for the week, but as soon as she walked into the fourth-grade room, she was too excited to think. There were Emma and Sam! Friends! And she saw Ruth's long black beaded braids and...

"Are you ready for this, Gabs?" a familiar, booming voice butted in enthusiastically.

Billy.

"Ready for what?" Abigail asked. If one thing was going to change in kids' club, she had hoped Billy would be less... Billy-like! It wasn't that she didn't like him—he wasn't mean or anything. They even had lots of fun together sometimes. But Billy didn't always know when enough was enough. And he was the only person in the whole world who insisted on calling her "Gabs"! **BLEH.** Abigail shuddered, suddenly worrying that Billy might have memorized the verse already. He loved to win.

CLAP! CLAP!

"Hi, everyone!" exclaimed a lady with dark hair and a big smile. "I'm your leader, Miss Shanner! Welcome to fourth-grade kids' club!"

As Miss Shanner high-fived everyone around the room, Abigail smiled to herself. Miss Shanner seemed nothing like Mrs. Hennig. Abigail finally felt like she knew where she was and what to do.

"Now, in fourth-grade club," Miss Shanner said, "we start with fun worksheets!"

A few people groaned.

"Hey now," Miss Shanner teased, "you don't know how cool fourth-grade kids'-club sheets are!" With a flourish, she held out some papers. "Here you go! I think you'll like these!"

Abigail sat in a creaky green plastic chair and grabbed a marker to start with. Glancing at the worksheet, she was relieved to see that it wasn't about the Peter story Mom had rushed through, or the memory verse. It was all about herself!

THUMP. Billy's elbow landed on the table next to Abigail's worksheet. He managed to make a lot of noise even when he was just reaching over for a marker.

"Your favorite thing about summer was swimming?" he teased competitively, peeking at Abigail's paper. "I bet you were in the kiddie pool, Gabs. I bet you didn't even go anywhere with waves or sharks like I did."

"I went to the lake at my cousin's," Abigail answered, leaving out the fact that she'd only swum in the pool *near* the lake. Fish and seaweed and lake stuff were gross!

"Well, *I* went to the ocean," Billy said proudly with a smile. "Are you done with blue?"

Abigail had to prove she'd had the most awesome summer. She handed him the blue marker and said, "I saw a shark." Never mind that it was in a tank at an aquarium.

"Me too," Billy grinned. But he looked like he was thinking really hard for a way to beat that. Taking the whole box of markers, he slowly said, "But, but, I bet you..."

CLAP! CLAP!

"Now we're going to toss this ball around," Miss Shanner explained enthusiastically as she held up a squishy orange ball. "When you catch it, say a fun fact about yourself."

Billy and Abigail's arms bumped hard as they both shot their hands straight up in the air, hoping for the ball.

"Hey!" Abigail exclaimed.

"I was first!" Billy announced. Abigail rolled her eyes. *Here we go*, she thought. *We were having fun, but Billy's going to take it too far!*

Without even looking at them, Miss Shanner tossed the ball right to Emma.

"My family has a parrot and he says woof like a dog," Emma said.

"I've been on nine planes," Ruth whispered shyly as she caught the ball, "and I'm nine."

"There are more than 4,000 varieties of potatoes in the world," Smarty-Pants Sam said on his turn, "and I'd like to try them all in my lifetime."

He tossed the ball right at Abigail.

WHAM! Billy's hand smashed into hers as he caught the ball first.

"I like to compete with Gabs in every game!" he

announced proudly, smiling at Abigail like she should be excited.

But Abigail just turned red and tried to laugh it off. Her arm hurt from all their bumping. She wished she was next to someone else.

"Sounds like Abby is good competition," Miss Shanner said lightly, with a reassuring wink at Abigail. "Now, Abby, what's your fun fact?"

Taking the ball from Billy's hands as she tried to think of something fast, Abigail blurted out, "Well, I just moved to a new house and new school." She threw the ball to someone else as quick as she could.

After everyone had had a turn, Miss Shanner took the ball back and said very dramatically, "So, who would like to know a fun fact about me?"

Abigail leaned in, forgetting for a minute about her annoyance with Billy because of the mysterious way Miss Shanner liked to say things.

"I... love..." Miss Shanner said, drawing out her words, "STORIES!"

Name:
Abigail Brenner

Age:
9

Favorite thing:
Swimming in Gracie's pool!

Craziest thing you did this summer:
move house and school

 Chapter Ten

Peter's Big Adventure

Abigail wanted to run up and hug Miss Shanner right there and then! Stories were the best! She couldn't wait to tell Miss Shanner her own stories—the ones she'd made up with her old friends.

"We're going to look at one of my favorite stories today," Miss Shanner said as she grabbed another stack of papers. "It's a really good story about... GRACE!"

Grace! That was what Dad said they needed lots of right now. Maybe Abigail was finally about to find out what it actually meant!

"Some of you might have started this story with your parents already if your family is doing the devotional book," Miss Shanner explained as she passed out papers. "But if you didn't, that's okay! It's optional!"

Abigail sighed with relief.

"We're going to spend a few weeks looking at the story of Peter, Jesus' friend," said Miss Shanner, "and seeing how his whole life changed when he met Jesus, who came to

save us! We're going to trace it on a timeline to see the big picture." She stretched her arms out wide. "Just like you made a big picture of your life a few minutes ago!"

Putting her hands to her face like she was peeking through binoculars, Miss Shanner added, "Then we'll look at some of the stories zoomed in."

Abigail cupped her hands around her eyes to look at the worksheet, like she was using binoculars too.

"Boring, right?" Billy muttered under his breath to Abigail as he popped the top off every single marker, dropping them back into the box one by one.

"Shh!" Abigail whispered. Billy couldn't take a hint. Didn't he see she was annoyed with him? But he was NOT going to ruin a good story for her. Especially not a story she'd been waiting for DAYS to hear the end of!

"When Peter got to know Jesus, his big adventure started with a job change and changing where he lived," Miss Shanner continued, nodding right at Abigail. "You know how it feels to move where you live, huh Abby?"

Nodding vigorously, Abigail pictured her cardboard-blocked bedroom and Greg's glaring face. "Yeah," she started to say, about to jump right into the whole story of everything that had happened so far in the Big Start Over. But Miss Shanner kept talking.

Crossing her arms, Abigail slid down into her seat. She tried to focus on Miss Shanner talking about the day everything changed for Peter.

"Our story starts *before* Peter met Jesus," Miss Shanner said. "Peter was a fisherman, and one day he was out fishing with his crew." She paused dramatically. "And what do you think they caught?"

"A bunch of trash!" Billy shouted excitedly,

apparently not bored at that idea. The pens in the box on his lap rattled and jumped.

"Fish, I would think," Sam said.

"I'm trying to remember," Abigail muttered at the same time, thinking about the super-fast way her mom had read it. She liked the way Miss Shanner was telling it better.

Laughing at the mess of noisy answers, Miss Shanner continued: "They caught... NOTHING!"

"They weren't very good fishermen, then," smirked Billy.

Miss Shanner shook her head and made her voice go all quiet. "Then Jesus came along. Jesus told Peter and his friends to drop their nets on the other side of the boat and..." She spread her arms all the way out. "Fish! So many squirmy, scaly fish that their nets broke!"

Abigail scrunched up her face. **ICK!** When were they getting to the good part?

"Peter couldn't believe it. It was a miracle! Only Jesus, the Son of God, could somehow get so many fish in one spot like that!" Miss Shanner exclaimed. "And what do you think Peter did?"

Finally, Abigail thought. They were going to find out what really happened between Peter and Jesus! Was this going to be the part where Peter messed up?

But before anyone could even raise a hand, Billy leapt up. "Is it game time yet?"

CRASH!

Too late, Abigail saw the whole box of open markers jump into the air as Billy moved. The pens sailed out of the box and flew right at...

GULP.

Right at Abigail. All those marker tips, right up against her light blue shirt. But now it wasn't just blue anymore.

She groaned. There were green marker squiggles and red marker lines and dark blue marker dots and yellow marker splotches all over her shirt! It was like the paint mess all over again! Mom was not going to be impressed... And now Abigail bet they wouldn't get to the end of the story... again.

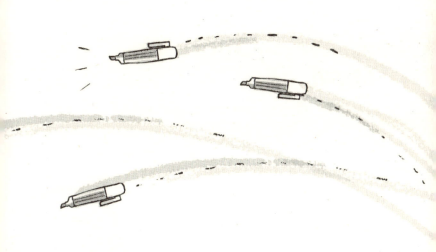

Chapter Eleven
Fisher of Men

"Billy, let's have a chat over here," Miss Shanner said, leading him to a corner. "You all turn over your worksheets and look at that memory verse for a few minutes, alright?" she told the rest of kids' club.

Abigail snatched up the open markers from her chair and the floor and used them to decorate all around the memory verse on the other side of her worksheet. "Grow in the grace and knowledge of our Lord and Savior Jesus Christ," she repeated inside.

Miss Shanner and Billy came back to the group, Billy thumping his elbows on the table next to Abigail so hard it bounced. Abigail shot him a look to tell him to stop it already, and then recited the whole verse one more time in her head.

"Grow in the grace and knowledge of our Lord and Savior Jesus Christ. Glory belongs to him both now and forever. Amen." 2 Peter chapter 3, verse 18. Inside her head she could say it superfast. *Please call on me first, Miss Shanner! Before I forget it!*

But Miss Shanner didn't remember to do the memory verse.

"Where was I?" she was saying instead, twisting the ends of her dark hair in her fingers. "Oh, right.

Peter was so amazed by Jesus after they caught all those fish that he said, 'Get away from me, Lord. I'm a sinner!'"

But... but... Miss Shanner must have skipped something! "Sinner" meant bad things, but Peter hadn't done anything bad! Besides being a gross fisherman, anyway. Why was he in trouble when he didn't do anything?

"Now, what made Peter a sinner?" Miss Shanner asked, like she was reading Abigail's mind. "Was he breaking lots of rules? What did he do so wrong?"

Abigail leaned in, ready for a real answer at last.

Smarty-Pants Sam raised his hand. When Miss Shanner called on him, he said, "Well, actually, sin isn't just breaking rules. It's doing things our way, not God's way. My mom told me."

"Your mom is a good teacher," Miss Shanner smiled. "Yes, Peter was a sinner like all of us are—he didn't do things God's way, and that got him into all sorts of messes. But Jesus was 100% perfect. He did EVERYTHING God's way. Peter didn't—he couldn't! So being with Jesus made him see how much of a mess he was."

Abigail crossed her arms again. That didn't seem very nice! If Jesus was so nice and loved people, like everybody always said, and if Jesus was so perfect that Peter felt bad about being a sinner when he was with him, then wouldn't Jesus be nice to Peter and be his friend?

Abigail shot her hand up to ask Miss Shanner, because she had to know! Did Peter and Jesus become friends or not? And how was this a grace story? And what even *was* grace?

KNOCK KNOCK! A grown-up appeared in the doorway with the third-grade group behind him. "Large group game time. Let's go!"

Abigail pumped her hand up higher. Was she never going to hear how the story ended?

But Miss Shanner said quickly, "Sorry, no time for questions. Here's what you need to know: Jesus gave Peter grace, which is like, umm... a second chance! He wanted to be friends with Peter even though Peter was a sinner. So Peter left his job as a fisherman so he could be with his friend Jesus. And Jesus gave him a new job—he told Peter he'd make him a fisher of people! Cool, right? We'll talk about that next week and see who memorized the Bible verse for the week and..."

But... but... Abigail thought again, her hand sinking down next to her and clutching her worksheet with the decorated memory verse and the timeline.

What is a fisher of people? she wondered as she followed her friends to the door. She felt bad for poor Peter as she imagined a guy catching people on fishing poles and walking them around with big old hooks. That would be a terrible adventure. Maybe even worse than Greg or the paint spill!

As Abigail got near the door, she tried to ask Miss Shanner if Peter and Jesus definitely did become friends and how to get second-chance grace and what "fisher of people" meant.

But Miss Shanner was quickly circling something on everyone's worksheets as they walked out.

"Look up this story this week," she said as Abigail held out her worksheet, "and next week bring a picture of something to represent it! Then we'll guess what it's about and keep tracing Peter's timeline to see how Jesus gives grace upon grace."

"Bet I can guess more than you, Gabs! And memorize more than you too!" Billy called out cheerily to Abigail as they bustled out the door.

"I already memorized the verse!" Abigail called back, feeling relieved about that at least. "Grow in grace—and grace means a second chance—and…" But Billy was already out of sight, running down the hallway. Annoyed, Abigail looked down at her stained shirt and added to herself, *AND I'm going to read ALL of these stories just so I can guess more than Billy!*

Grow in the grace and knowledge of our Lord and Savior Jesus Christ
2 Peter 3:18

Peter's Timeline:

By the Lake - Luke 5:1-5
A Huge Catch - Luke 5:5-10a
From Now On - Luke 5:9-11
At Peter's House - Matthew 8:14-17
A Furious Storm - Matthew 8:23-27
Who is Jesus? - Matthew 16:13-17
A Dark Night - Matthew 26:30-35
Soldiers! - John 18:1-5
Peter's Sword - John 18:10-14
The Rooster Crows - Luke 22:54-62
Gone - John 20: 1-10
Fish for Breakfast - John 21:4-13
Feeding Sheep - John 21:15-17
A Strange Sound - Acts 1:8-9
Peter's Message - Acts 2:38-41

Draw how you imagine Peter looked...

Peter's other name:

Peter's hometown:

Peter's job:

Next week, bring a picture or an object to represent the story circled for you!

★ Chapter Twelve

Nana and Grandpa's

Of course, Abigail's parents were too busy to look up any of the stories about Peter with her that night. She just sighed as they gave her a quick hug goodnight—on the couch. Again.

In the morning, there was a different important thing she couldn't find in her backpack on the bus. This time, it was her Amazing Adventure Box! She had promised Flora and the other kids they'd finish their game, and now they wouldn't be able to. **UGH!**

But nobody remembered the game at lunch

time anyway. And Flora didn't even listen long enough to hear one of Abigail's stories after saying hi. She just talked to everybody… and talked… and talked… and everybody listened because Flora was cool. With her Amazing Adventure Box missing, Abigail was just…

"Hey, headband." Again.

I thought this Big Start Over was getting better, she sighed as she got a whiff of fishsticks in the cafeteria. *But maybe my adventure is lame like Peter's. Fisher of people.* **ICK.**

At least she was getting picked up by Dad instead of going home on the bus today. "Hey Abby-girl!" Dad said as she climbed into his truck after school. "Guess what? You might get to go to Nana and Grandpa's!"

"NANA and GRANDPA'S!" Abigail repeated in a happy shout. That made the whole crummy week better! Their house was one place that never, ever changed and was always an adventure. Mom even said the brightly colored decorations and wacky pictures were the exact same as when she was a kid, and that was a very long time ago.

"Thought you'd like that," Dad teased. "Can you check my phone, please? I'm waiting for a text back to see if they're home first."

Abigail squinted at the phone screen, wondering where else they would be. Nana never checked her phone fast, so waiting to hear back just seemed silly!

"Yes, I can go," Abigail said, even though there was no message. Why wouldn't Nana and Grandpa want her to come over? They were always happy to see her! Just like Mom used to be...

RINNNGGG!

"Mom's calling," Abigail said, tapping the speaker button.

"Hank?" Mom said to Dad, "I need more paint,

but the store closes crazy early. It's on the other side of town." Mom still sounded very stressed. "Abby can't sleep in her room until…"

"Abby's with me!" Dad said quickly.

"Oh," Mom said.

Oh? Just oh? Not even hi? Abigail hoped Dad wouldn't see her cheeks turn red. She guessed Mom was really mad about the paint mess still. And the shirt Billy ruined. It wasn't fair! It wasn't Abigail's fault!

CRUNCH. They pulled into her grandparents' driveway, and Abigail waved quickly as she hopped out. Dad hardly seemed to notice. He backed up as soon as the door of the truck shut.

Abigail trotted eagerly up to the pretty blue front door of her grandparents' home. A good Nana snack and Grandpa story would make everything okay. She turned the knob and gave it a push, opening her mouth to yell, "Helllllloooo…"

But her words got stuck.

The door didn't open.

The knob didn't click.

It was locked.

GULP.

Maybe Nana and Grandpa weren't actually home. But where else would they be? What did nanas and grandpas do besides make snacks and tell jokes and swap stories? Abigail's

grandparents' door was never locked. What should she do?

KNOCK, KNOCK, KNOCK. She pounded on the door.

"Hellllooooo!" she called out.

As she thudded her fist against the bright blue door, Abigail felt her heart thud too. Nana and Grandpa's house wasn't as inviting when it was locked. Where *were* they?

Then Abigail had an idea. Mom did always say they were "hard of hearing." They probably just couldn't hear her right now. Abigail figured she

just needed to go around to the back door.

Racing around the garage to the back fence, she found that the big, wooden gate was shut. She jiggled its handle, but it was locked too!

Even though she'd been there a million times and her grandparents said the neighbors were nice, Abigail felt like there was a big old rock in her stomach. When had all the houses in this neighborhood got so huge… and dark? Some scary stranger might be watching her!

With a squeak, Abigail squished herself in the bushes to hide. They prickled and stung, but then she noticed: there was a gap in the fence behind them!

Squeezing tight, Abigail prayed she wouldn't ruin yet another new school shirt as she pushed through the pokey bush into the backyard.

"Ow!" she exclaimed as she fell onto the grass behind the fence. Her white shorts were now green. Her arms were red. Abigail was all scratched up, and some spots on her hands and wrists were bleeding a little.

She took a deep breath. She was NOT going to cry.

⭐ Chapter Thirteen

Sticky-Duct-Aids

"You're a fourth-grader," Abigail said out loud to herself. "Plus, you're the grown-up right now, and a grown-up would put band-aids over all these scratches."

The back garage door turned out to be unlocked, thankfully, but the door from the garage into the house wasn't. Abigail carefully climbed over Grandpa's tools and stuff. Once, a meow spooked her, but she figured her grandparents' cat, Snickers, was in there somewhere saying hi. Snickers loved to play hide and seek.

Looking in Grandpa's drawers and on all the shelves that were low enough to see, she didn't find any band-aids. But she did see duct tape and some big scissors.

Grandpa always said duct tape could fix anything.

Carefully peeling back some of the silvery, sticky stuff from the roll, Abigail slowly cut off a bunch of tiny strips. The thought of peeling duct tape off her little cuts sounded painful, so she grabbed some scrap paper and chopped some of them into band-aid-size bits. She wrote all the words that popped into her head on them, to decorate them like the cool cartoon band-aids Mom bought sometimes. They wouldn't be as cool as if she had her rainbow sticky notes and multi-pen from her Amazing Adventure Box, of course. If only she hadn't lost it! But at least this was something.

When she'd stuck each little piece of tape and paper over her scratches and scrapes, all up and down her arms, Abigail said out loud, "We'll call these... sticky-duct-aids!"

THUMP.
CRASH!
WHEEEE...

"Ahhh!" Abigail screamed and jumped as she heard loud noises outside all of a sudden. She crouched behind a stack of tall plastic buckets and closed her eyes. Was it going to be scary strangers? Who had seen her go into the garage?

But then there was light. The big door was opening!

"Grandpa! Nana!" Abigail yelled. She rushed out from behind the buckets toward the driveway.

THUNK. Oh no! Abigail's knee had knocked into the tower of buckets. The top one toppled off, the lid bouncing away... Another one followed...

SSSSSS...

The buckets were full of birdseed.

Well, they *had* been full of birdseed.

Nana's jaw fell open as she climbed out of the car in front of the garage and found Abigail surrounded by the little seeds and kernels.

"Abigail?" she exclaimed. "What happened? What's going on?" Nana rushed toward her.

"Mac!" Nana yelled to Grandpa. "Can you grab a broom?" She looked back up from the mess to Abigail. "Honey, what's going on? Why are you in our garage?" She paused. "*How* did you get in the garage?"

"Well," Abigail started, blushing. She'd have to tell the whole story. "Well, the other night Mom was real stressed, and Dad, and Henry made this huge mess..."

"Abby-girl, let's skip to the garage part, okay?" Nana interrupted as Grandpa came and started sweeping up the birdseed. He winked at Abigail without saying a word.

"I climbed through the bushes when Dad dropped me off," she said, feeling more confident, "because you weren't home, so I had to come in through the back door... and... and..."

Abigail looked again at her Nana's face. Nana hated messes.

"Snickers knocked those buckets over!" Abigail lied. Blaming her grandparents' cat was bad, but she didn't want to get in trouble again! Besides, she *had* heard Snickers when she got into the garage. And Snickers was always knocking stuff over. It could have been true.

"Snickers?" Nana said, looking at the wide open doors. Then Nana practically shouted, "Snickers! Mac! The cat was in the garage!"

Uh oh. Snickers wasn't supposed to be in the garage because then she might escape outside and get lost!

While Grandpa finished clearing up the birdseed, Abigail and Nana searched high and low in the garage and all through the yard. But there was no sign of Snickers.

"She must have run outside," Nana said worriedly. "She must be lost!"

"Lost?" Abigail gulped, rubbing her aching stomach. This was NOT the kind of adventure she'd been hoping for! She squeezed her Nana's hand, filled with all the sorriest feelings.

"It'll be okay," Nana said, patting her head. "We'll find her!"

"But it's my fault, it's my fault," Abigail said.

Nana shook her head. "Cats are like this. There's grace enough, Abby-girl. Don't worry about letting her out."

But what if I lost her forever? Abigail worried. *What if my adventure story doesn't have a happy ending for Snickers?*

"Snicky, Snicks, Snicker, Snickers!" she called one more time, trying to think of the nicest ways to say the cat's name. Snickers was a big, fluffy calico cat with lots of colors and a noisy, scratchy purr. When Abigail was smaller, Snickers had never even hissed if Abigail had pulled her tail or accidentally petted her the wrong way. Abigail's head hurt thinking Snickers might be lost all because of her.

"I'm sorry, Nana," she whispered again. "I didn't mean to…"

"I know," Nana said. "Besides, you're just a girl. It's your dad who's in big trouble for leaving you here alone!"

Abigail gulped. But she couldn't admit that that was her fault too.

When Mom arrived, she was so grumpy about Abigail being there alone and covered in sticky-duct-aids and torn-up, dirty, bush-covered clothes, and Snickers getting lost, that she talked to no one in particular all the way home.

"All we need," she said to the steering wheel, "is for one more thing to go wrong."

"So much for a nice surprise tonight," she

told the car door as she got out and slammed it shut. "Again."

"Another load of laundry," she complained to the front door of the house. "I'm on my last soap pod, and it hasn't even been a week!"

Just before the front door opened, there was a huge crack of thunder, and it started to rain.

"Great," said Mom.

Abigail didn't say anything. She just wished this week was over.

 Chapter Fourteen

Walking on Water

"Uh oh," Henry said as his lip quivered while he watched Abigail tear off her sticky-duct-aids carefully and put on the real band-aids Mom had found for her. They were cool animal ones, but tears stung at Abigail's eyes anyway.

Henry suddenly ran out of the bathroom, but Abigail hardly noticed. The tears welled up extra when she peeled the "grow in grace" sticky-duct-aid off.

"How do I even grow in grace like that memory verse says?" she whispered, feeling the burn of the tape pulling her arm hairs up.

"Miss Shanner said Jesus gave grace to Peter after he said he was a sinner. Grace is like a second chance," she muttered as she stuck a duck band-aid on.

"Second means two," she worried as she pulled off the "I ♥ Snickers" sticky-duct-aid and wondered if she'd ever see her furry friend again. "I messed up more than two times this week."

She stuck on a fresh band-aid with a fish on it. "How many chances do I get, God?" she prayed.

"Gabigaa," Henry said nicely as he reappeared, holding up her glittery Amazing Adventure Box. "Bett-ah?"

"My box!" Abigail exclaimed, reaching out to

hug it. Henry clung to it too, leaning right in to be part of the hug. "Where'd you find it?"

Whatever Henry explained in his toddler babble, Abigail couldn't understand. But she could understand that he wanted to make something cool together again. Looking down at the fish band-aid she'd just stuck on, Abigail knew just what special thing she and Henry could do.

"Come on, Henry," she said, heading for the couch. Right next to it, she found their family Bible and the orange book they were supposed to read all together. The papers from kids' club were tucked inside.

"Since Mom and Dad are too busy for anything," Abigail said, feeling grown-up, "you and me are going to do the kids'-club project all on our own, Henry! And we're going to do a better job than Billy!"

Henry clapped his hands. Abigail chuckled

as she handed him some sticky notes and her multi-pen and told him to take good notes for her.

She squinted at the little spot Miss Shanner had circled for her. Matthew 14:22-33, it said. Careful with the big heavy Bible, she flipped through until she saw "Matthew" in the top corner of a page. Then she turned the pages, reading out some headlines along the way, like Dad always did. "Jesus Chooses His First Disciples. Jesus Heals Many People. Jesus Sends Out the Twelve Disciples."

"Peter had a Big Start Over too, like us," she explained to Henry in her best teachery voice. "He left his home and changed jobs just so that he could follow Jesus and be his friend. All the stories on Miss Shanner's timeline are about Peter's friendship with Jesus, I think."

At last she saw a big, dark 14 on the page. She looked for the little numbers for the verse, just like Mom had taught her back before she was so busy all the time. When she found the little 22, she looked at Henry, cleared her throat very seriously, and started to read out loud in her best grown-up voice.

Jesus Walks on Water

²² Right away Jesus made the disciples get into the boat. He had them go on ahead of him to the other side of the Sea of Galilee. Then he sent the crowd away. ²³ After he had sent them away, he went up on a mountainside by himself to pray. Later that night, he was there alone. ²⁴ The boat was already a long way from land. It was being pounded by the waves because the wind was blowing against it.

²⁵ Shortly before dawn, Jesus went out to the disciples. He walked on the lake. ²⁶ They saw him walking on the lake and were terrified. "It's a ghost!" they said. And they cried out in fear.

²⁷ Right away Jesus called out to them, "Be brave! It is I. Don't be afraid."

²⁸ "Lord, is it you?" Peter asked. "If it is, tell me to come to you on the water."

²⁹ "Come," Jesus said.

So Peter got out of the boat. He walked on the water toward Jesus. ³⁰ But when Peter saw the wind, he was afraid. He began to sink. He cried out, "Lord! Save me!"

³¹ Right away Jesus reached out his hand and caught him. "Your faith is so small!" he said. "Why did you doubt me?"

³² When they climbed into the boat, the wind died down. ³³ Then those in the boat worshiped Jesus. They said, "You really are the Son of God!"

Henry shuddered when Abigail made "whooshing" sounds for the wind and waves, waving her arms. It helped that it was gray and windy outside the window already. His eyes got big when she read, "It's a ghoooost!" When Jesus said it was just him, Henry breathed a sigh of relief.

But when Peter walked out there on the water, with Abigail wiggling to shake the sofa cushions like they were on the waves too, Henry's hand shook hard, making the multi-pen tap, tap, tap against a sticky note. Guiltily, Abigail remembered that *she* hadn't liked the idea of the lake that summer because of the fish and all that… but Henry wouldn't even get in the pool!

"Uh oh!" Henry started to say, his lip trembling, "Uh oh!" Outside, the rain was falling harder and harder.

Abigail felt a bit like saying "Uh oh" too.

Peter's Big Start Over was... yikes! Thinking Jesus was a ghost? And then walking on water to reach him? And then almost drowning? Abigail only half paid attention as she hurried to read the rest. *I really don't know if I like this adventure story. I thought Jesus was supposed to help since he is God!*

"Jesus reached out his hand and caught him!" Abigail read, and then reread, patting Henry's hand like Mom would to make him feel better.

"Why did you doubt me?" she read. That was what Jesus said to Peter. Abigail narrowed her eyes. Was this the moment when Peter messed up? He'd doubted Jesus. Abigail knew what doubt meant: it meant not believing. Peter had got scared instead of trusting Jesus. He'd used up his second chance, just like Abigail! Surely Jesus wasn't going to forgive Peter AGAIN?

BOOM. Thunder cracked outside, and Abigail couldn't tell if the rain was louder or Henry's scream. He leapt off the couch, dropped her multi-pen on the floor with a thunk, and ran for Mom.

"Oh no!" Abigail sighed as she heard Henry run and run through the house, yelling "Maa-ma! Maa-ma!" *You weren't supposed to scare your little brother with Bible stories.* She had got it wrong again.

Sad and confused, Abigail scratched at the band-aids dotting her arms. When her fingernail caught on the one with a cat, she felt even worse. Snickers. Poor Snickers hated water even more than Henry. She wouldn't even go near a sink!

"And it's raining so hard," Abigail whispered.

Was Snickers all wet and feeling like she was going to drown, like Peter almost did? What if she came back and never wanted Abigail to pet her again? Could cats change their mind about loving you if you messed up too much?

"Urrrrrgh," Abigail heard Mom moan to herself in the hallway. "Just what I needed tonight. A screaming toddler."

Abigail closed her eyes and asked God two questions in her head. *Did you give Peter more than two chances?* And, *Please can there be enough grace for me still?*

⭐ Chapter Fifteen
Greg Again

The next morning Abigail looked out for Flora's dark curls and trademark brightly colored clothing, hoping to tell her about Snickers and ask for help making a lost cat poster at lunch. But she only saw Flora right outside the classroom, and they didn't have a chance to say anything except hello.

All morning long, Abigail wondered if Snickers was okay. She tried to pay attention to Mrs. Hennig, but Snickers' splotchy, fluffy little face kept popping into her head, wet from all the rain outside.

She brought her multi-pen and some big pieces of paper ripped out of her spiral notebook to lunch to make a Lost Snickers poster with Flora.

But when she got to the table, lots of other kids were already sitting with Flora. And Flora was telling them lots of things. She didn't even seem to notice Abigail was missing.

1, 2, 3, 4, 5, 6. That was how many kids Abigail counted sitting between her and Flora. *And who's next to me?* she thought miserably. *Greg. He won't even look at me. He isn't even talking to anybody.*

Abigail scribbled silently on the big, lined sheets of notebook paper as she chewed her sandwich. Every few minutes, she leaned around Greg's dark-haired head to peek down to the end of the table. Surely Flora would be looking for her! But Flora was laughing and

talking, and all the kids near her looked just as happy.

Feeling forgotten, Abigail winced at the sting behind her eyes and the growing ache in her stomach. Were they still going to go on their park adventure tomorrow? Maybe she didn't even want to go with Flora when she had forgotten about her so fast...

"Flora's good at making friends, huh?" Greg suddenly asked, still not looking at Abigail.

"Yeah," Abigail said, trying not to sound too sad in front of the class bully as her cheeks turned red.

"I thought you two were friends," Greg observed through a mouthful of food. "Like best friends."

I thought so too, Abigail sighed inside. But she just focused on her lost cat poster and ignored him. *Maybe I should make a lost friend poster while I'm at it*, she thought.

"So what happened? Why are you sitting so far away?" Greg pressed on.

Abigail's poster got all blurry as her eyes filled with tears. She tried to squint hard to keep them inside.

"Why do you want to know?" she said through clenched teeth.

"What's that?" Greg asked, leaning closer to look at her poster and dripping sauce from his slimy fingers on the paper. "A cat or something?"

Or something?! Abigail thought, looking at her sauce-stained sketch. "It's none of your business!" All of her hurt feelings were suddenly boiling up inside.

"Here," Greg said, excitedly grabbing her multi-pen out of her hand, "let me draw too!"

BOOM.

Abigail practically heard it in her ears, even though it was somewhere deep inside. It felt like something had exploded in her heart as she slid back her heavy rust-red chair, nearly knocking it over.

"We're not friends!" she exclaimed at Greg.

"No one even likes you!"

She didn't have time to notice his face or if he said anything back. The whole room got swirly, like she was Peter drowning in the sea.

BLEGGGGGHHH!

Abigail's days-old stomach ache moved up. And up. And out onto the cafeteria floor. Just like she was on a boat, Abigail bent right over and lost her lunch everywhere.

A bunch of teachers she didn't know rushed to her rescue, and she could barely hear all the "Ew!" and "Gross!" exclamations of the other kids—the grown-ups were all talking at once.

"Call the nurse!"

"I'll just walk her there!"

"Can you walk, hon?"

"Were you feeling sick all day?"

Soon, the school nurse was writing stuff down as she held up the thermometer.

BEEP BEEP BEEP!

"Hmm," the nurse said, "no fever."

She kept asking all sorts of questions, right up until Abigail finally heard a grown-up voice she knew.

"Abby?"

Please don't be mad at me for another mess! Abigail panicked. But Mom just wrapped an arm around her shoulders.

"Let's go home, Abby-girl," Mom said softly.

Chapter Sixteen
We Need to Talk

"You'll feel better soon," Mom reassured Abigail on the way home.

"I'm not really sick, I don't think," Abigail said, feeling bad that she felt bad. Everything had just been too much, and she had felt so upset and so yucky. She couldn't believe she'd barfed in the cafeteria in front of everyone!

Nodding, Mom said, "I think I know what's wrong."

GULP. Abigail wondered guiltily just how much her Mom knew. Did she know that

Abigail had been mean to Greg, and that she'd spilled the birdseed in Nana and Grandpa's garage and lost Snickers FOREVER, and that she'd already lost her only new friend at school? Did Mom know what a big mess Abigail had made out of the Big Start Over? And that she'd used up all of God's grace?

WHIFF... Walking into the front door of the house that still didn't feel like home, Abigail thought she smelled peanut butter cookies. But that didn't make sense! Mom was too busy to bake anymore.

Abigail's achy stomach rumbled hungrily despite the cafeteria incident. She went straight into the kitchen, with Mom right behind her.

The boxes were all gone.

Dad's silly giant dinosaur spoon was hanging off the fridge.

Mom's favorite flowers—bright yellow

tulips—were on
the table.

So was a plate
of the best-ever
peanut butter
cookies!

"Hey, Abby-girl," Mom said softly as Abigail eyed the cookies on top of the oven. "Cookies probably aren't the best choice when your tummy hurts."

Abigail nodded, still in shock at how normal everything seemed.

"Henry's with Nana, so it's just you and me," Mom added, not even sounding stressed about anything.

Was this a dream? Or was all the bad stuff a dream? *Dear God*, Abigail prayed, *please, please, please can this be the week starting again, except awesome this time?*

"We need to talk," Mom said.

Abigail sighed. It wasn't a dream. "We need to talk" was grown-up for "You're in trouble, missy."

Mom took a seat at the table, facing right toward Abigail.

GULP.

"So, Abby-girl," Mom started to say, very seriously.

"Sooo," Abigail butted in, her eyes welling up with tears again. "I know. I know. I messed up this whole adventure, and I didn't do the Big Start Over right. And I made big messes. And I ruined my clothes. And I lied about Nana saying I could come. And everyone is disappointed in me! And the kids in my class don't like me. And I used up all God's grace. And I scared Henry with the Bible, and I let Sn—"

"Abby, Abby," Mom interrupted, rushing forward off her chair to give her a hug. "Abby-girl, you're not in trouble."

"I'm not?" Abigail said, so surprised her tears stopped.

"No," Mom said, "I was going to tell you, Abby-girl, that I'm sorry!"

Mom was sorry?

All the words fell right out of Abigail's brain.

Giving her another hug, Mom said, "I have been so stressed about getting the house ready that I have not been patient. Or kind. Or gentle. I've stressed you out so much you lost your lunch, poor girl. And..."

Mom paused, shaking her head.

"Figure this one out," she said, sighing. "I was trying to make this house home for you. I was trying to surprise you with the most awesome Adventure Central ever... and instead, remember? I got mad at you about the paint and didn't take any time for you! I'm so sorry, Abby."

Abigail's mind was racing. She knew she hadn't been patient or kind or gentle either...

but she'd done much worse. She'd lost Snickers!

"Come here," Mom said gently, tugging Abigail's hand toward the hallway.

There weren't any boxes in the hallway either!

And there was a picture of her and Henry on the wall!

"Close your eyes, Miss," Mom said playfully.

Abigail shut both eyes really hard. Mom's hands on her shoulders guided her where to walk since she couldn't see. *I need to remember to add this for a game idea to Adventure Central,* Abigail thought. *Wait... Adventure Central... we're walking toward my room...*

Was it... was it ready? Was this happening? Mom hadn't forgotten?

Abigail could hardly keep her eyes shut anymore. Mom yelled, "Open them!"

Abigail saw...

Purple. Blue. Orange. Yellow.

Dots! Squares! Clouds!

On the walls!

Big and small!

Some overlapped, some stood alone, but they were everywhere. It was like walking into an adventure. There was so much to see!

"This is way better than a bulletin board!" Abigail yelled, bouncing up and down on her toes. "It's so pretty, Mom! It looks... it looks like I'm in a painting, or on a secret planet made of shapes, or in a fancy magical candy store where you can climb up the colors on the walls or, or... I don't know!"

"You can imagine all day in here," Mom smiled, "and do you want to know the best part?"

"There's more?" Abigail squealed, hardly even knowing what to do as she gazed happily at purple triangles bigger than her whole body and orange clouds which she imagined tasted like dreamsicle ice cream.

Chapter Seventeen

Adventure Central

Grabbing something off Abigail's desk, Mom walked up to the wall, and then looked back over her shoulder. She made a guilty face like she was a very naughty little puppy, and drew...

On.

The.

Wall.

"Mom!" Abigail yelled. "What are you doing? You're going to ruin..."

Mom interrupted with a big laugh and handed Abigail a piece of chalk.

"Every colorful shape is chalk paint... like a blackboard!" she smiled.

"Sooo..." Abigail finished, "I can write on them? I can write on the walls? And it'll rub off and be good as new again?"

"You can fill Adventure Central—your whole room, every wall—with all your games and dreams and stories and sketches." Mom swept an arm around the room. "All your best ideas for adventures can live here, Abby-miss-creative-girl."

"Wow!" was the only thing Abigail could think of to say.

"And here," Mom laughed, handing her a little box. "You can add these glittery multicolored chalk sticks to your Amazing Adventure Box."

Racing out of the room to her backpack

to grab her shiny box and then right back to Adventure Central, Abigail opened it up to make room for her new chalk. But as the box lid opened up, Abigail saw a piece of notebook paper shoved inside.

Her drawing of Snickers stared back at her. She was still missing!

She lifted up that paper and found two sticky notes underneath, covered in Henry's squiggles and pen scratches. He had been so scared by the story about Peter!

Just then, she felt her Mom's arm around her. "So, what do you think of Adventure Central?" Mom asked. "Does it make this Big Start Over feel less like a Big Mess?"

But Abigail didn't feel better. Or excited. Not right then. She felt like running away from Mom, who was being so nice even after all Abigail's mess-ups. *Get away from me!* she thought. *I don't deserve this!*

Her mouth fell open. *Oh no! This is just like that story...*

"Mom?" Abigail said, pulling away and quickly closing her Amazing Adventure Box without even fitting her glittery new chalk inside. "I'm a... I'm a... a sinner! Like Peter!"

"Like Peter?" Mom said in a confused voice as she sat down on Abigail's favorite purple blanket on her bed and patted the spot next to her. Abigail slid next to her, taking a deep breath.

"In kids' club we learned about how Jesus was being really kind to Peter—just like you're being to me," Abigail explained. "But Peter told Jesus to go away because he knew he was a sinner. Just like me."

"I see..." Mom said, rubbing her chin like she was actually still trying to figure it out.

"And Mom," Abigail said, "when Henry was scared the other night? That was me too. I read him the Bible story from my kids' club project—you know, the one where Peter doubted Jesus and almost drowned? I even messed up the Bible, Mom! I messed up this whole Big Start Over! You don't even know..."

"Mmm," Mom said, nodding like maybe she was getting it. "We have a lot of catching up to do for the week, huh? How about you start at the beginning?"

Abigail sighed. "I wish I could just start over at the beginning. But it's too late."

Mom put her arm around Abigail again and gave her a squeeze. "It's never too late to start over," she said firmly. "Not in the things that are the most important, anyway. God's grace is enough for us to start over again and again."

"Nana said that about grace too," Abigail remembered. "But Mom, I don't get it. Miss Shanner said that Peter's story is a good grace story, and he got a second chance, but I used up lots of chances already, and so did he, I think. Did Jesus really keep forgiving Peter when he kept messing up all the time?"

Abigail's words tumbled out so fast and so hard she couldn't even keep track of what she was saying. She told Mom everything she could think of about the past week. How hurt her

feelings were when Mom wasn't listening. How she was nervous about school and didn't know anybody and her teacher was very strict. How she and Greg didn't start off very good, and then she was mean to him. And she thought Flora was her friend, but then Flora forgot all about her. And it was Henry who spilled the paint—she just found it. But it was her fault in Grandpa's garage, and she had lied to Dad, and Snickers was lost…

"Abby-girl," Mom interrupted her, "I'm sorry, I forgot to tell you! They found Snickers in the house right after we left! She was never lost to begin with."

"What?" Abigail cried with a big sigh of relief. She could finally take a deep breath again, picturing Snickers' orange and white and brown fluffy face purring on Nana's lap. Except… "Well, well… that's just one thing that wasn't so bad then… but Mom?"

"Yes?" Mom said, looking like she was thinking really hard.

"I'm sorry, because I messed up A LOT," Abigail said. Her stomach started to hurt again. Her eyes started to get wet. All the feelings hit, all at once.

⭐ Chapter Eighteen
A Good Grace Story

"Be right back," Mom said softly, darting out of the room. Soon she plopped back down on the bed, holding a big pile of stuff: the family Bible, the kids' club papers, and the orange book the family was supposed to be reading together. Mom tapped the orange book.

"I'm sorry I rushed this the other day and that the story got confusing. We're going to sort it out! But right now," Mom said, flipping through the family Bible and smiling, "I want to show you what I think Miss Shanner is getting at.

This IS a good grace story! And yours is too!"

Biting her lip, Abigail looked at Mom doubtfully.

"So here's the thing," Mom said. "Peter messed up. A lot. He was a sinner. Like you and like me." She pointed at Abigail and herself. "But Jesus forgives us when we come to him. He gives us grace—which means he lets us start over and over and over again, because our adventures are WITH Jesus. All these stories about Peter are part of one big story, Abby-girl, about Jesus and how good he is!"

Mom patted Abigail on the hand. "Guess what?" she said. "One time, Peter even lied and said he didn't know Jesus—three times!—when Jesus really needed a good friend because he was going to die on the cross. That was a real mess-up. The worst."

Abigail nodded. She knew what it was like to really need a good friend.

Mom continued, "And you know what? Jesus already knew Peter would abandon him. And he knew everything you would do wrong too, Abby. And everything I would do wrong! But Jesus went to the cross to die to save us—including Peter—anyway!"

"Why would he do that?" Abigail asked.

"Because that's who Jesus is," Mom said, nudging her shoulder gently. "His love for us and his grace to us never run out. So it's never too late to start over! You know, after Peter lied about knowing Jesus, Jesus died and rose from the grave, and guess what happened next?"

Before Abigail could answer, Mom excitedly tapped the Bible page and started reading a story that sounded just like the one they'd rushed through the other night.

Fishing. **ICK.** No catches. **WHEW.** Then Jesus said what to do, and Peter and his friends suddenly caught loads of fish. Gross.

"Jesus said to them, 'Come and have breakfast,'" Mom read.

Abigail frowned. "I don't remember this part."

Mom's eyes twinkled. "It sounded just like that story you learned about when Jesus changed Peter's whole life and asked him to be a fisher of people, right? Until the breakfast part?"

"Yeah," Abigail nodded.

"Well," Mom said, grinning, "this story is actually three years AFTER that one! Jesus gave Peter the Big Start Over of becoming his friend. Peter messed up lots, and Jesus forgave him again and again, and then Peter lied, and Jesus died on the cross to save us, and Jesus rose from the dead. THEN this happened."

"Oh," Abigail realized, "this is a new story. But it has the same start." Her eyes got big. "It's like... starting Peter and Jesus' adventure-grace-story all over again!"

"Yes!" Mom's smile was huge as she read

the rest. "See," she said when she was done, "because of who Jesus is and how much grace he gives when we sin, it's NEVER too late to start over again with him."

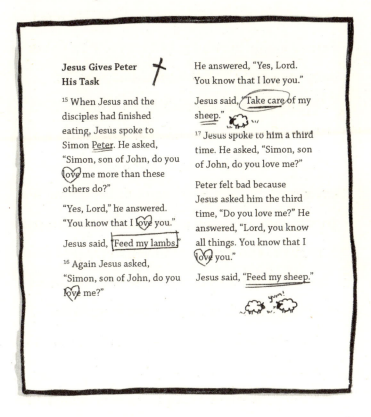

Jesus Gives Peter His Task

¹⁵ When Jesus and the disciples had finished eating, Jesus spoke to Simon Peter. He asked, "Simon, son of John, do you love me more than these others do?"

"Yes, Lord," he answered. "You know that I love you."

Jesus said, "Feed my lambs."

¹⁶ Again Jesus asked, "Simon, son of John, do you love me?"

He answered, "Yes, Lord. You know that I love you."

Jesus said, "Take care of my sheep."

¹⁷ Jesus spoke to him a third time. He asked, "Simon, son of John, do you love me?"

Peter felt bad because Jesus asked him the third time, "Do you love me?" He answered, "Lord, you know all things. You know that I love you."

Jesus said, "Feed my sheep."

"Jesus forgave Peter," Mom explained, smiling wide. "He showed Peter grace and let him start over again! He got a very special job from Jesus!"

"Oh!" Abigail said, putting all the pieces together as she remembered Peter's first Big Start Over. "That's a fisher of people! But that sounds... icky..."

Mom laughed. "That was in the first story. This time Jesus told him he was going to be a feeder of God's sheep."

"Sheep?" Abigail waggled her eyebrows, all confused.

Mom smiled. "Being a fisher of people means Peter got to tell people about Jesus and his forgiveness, so they could start over and follow Jesus too. And then being a feeder of sheep means Peter got to help Jesus' followers keep growing in grace."

"That's good news!" Abigail said, "Because, because..."

"Because you can't use up God's grace, Abby-girl," Mom smiled. "Remember, your Big Start Over right now is part of Jesus' big, awesome grace adventure story. It's a good story! Jesus can help you start over in this part of your story too."

"Really?"

"Yup, grace is a free gift we don't deserve," Mom said. "A free gift God gives us through Jesus. And, when we follow Jesus, grace is a gift we can give each other as well. And I want to give it you, Abby-girl. I forgive you for the lying and mess-ups this week. Do you think you can forgive me too? For all my bad attitude?"

"Yes! I forgive you," Abigail said at once, squeezing Mom into a tight hug.

"There you go!" Mom said. "That's grace you just gave me too, Abby-girl! We started over with each other!"

"It really is the Big Start Over, like Dad said!" Abigail giggled.

"And the Big Mess, like I said," Mom chuckled. "It can be both, and be a good story, with grace."

Scooting off her bed, Abigail slipped a silvery-blue stick of chalk out of the pack and started to write in the nearest purple circle on the wall.

"Abigail's Big Messy Grace Start Over Adventure with Jesus," she scrawled, slowly reading the words out to Mom as she wrote them.

"That sounds like a good story," Mom said.

"Does this adventure have a happy ending?"

"I don't know..." Abigail admitted, turning around. "What about school? And Greg? And Flora?"

"Let's think about God's grace in all that too," Mom said gently, "but first, how about we pray and ask for God's forgiveness for both of our sin messes this week, and ask for his help starting over on this adventure, okay? And maybe we can practice your memory verse together then? I think I remember it was about grace too..."

Grow in the Grace and knowledge of our Lord and Savior Jesus Christ –

2 Peter 3:18

Chapter Nineteen

Fantastic Flora

When Abigail walked into Corolla Elementary the next day, she felt ten times lighter, even though her stomach was full of peanut butter cookies from the night before.

She looked for Flora nervously, hoping that Mom was right—that if Abigail gave Flora grace, maybe they could still be friends.

But Abigail didn't see Flora at all. What she did see once she sat down were the plain gray shoes of Mrs. Hennig suddenly next to her desk.

GULP. Abigail's mind raced with all the reasons why she could be in trouble.

"Miss Brenner," Mrs. Hennig said almost-happily, "I'm glad you're feeling better. Greg said you left this behind yesterday, so I've been keeping it for you. It looks very snazzy."

CLINK! Abigail's multi-pen rattled on the desk for a second. She hadn't even realized it was lost! She smiled up at her teacher with big, amazed eyes. Maybe Mrs. Hennig wasn't as bad as she'd thought.

RINNNGGG!

That was the school bell. Pulling out her math workbook, Abigail clicked her pen to orange.

Maybe if she used one of her favorite colors, math wouldn't be so bad.

Out of the corner of her eye, she noticed someone looking at her. Greg.

He was scrunching up his nose, widening his bright blue eyes, and scrunching his mouth to make a ridiculous face at her.

SIGH. It seemed Abigail still had an enemy. But maybe that wouldn't be so bad if she had a friend too. Where had Flora gone anyway?

Abigail tried not to look at Greg through math. Or spelling. Or reading. Finally...

RINNNGGG!

Lunchtime. *Here we go,* Abigail sighed inside, trying to work up her courage like Mom said. *Please God, can "Grow in the grace and knowledge of our Lord and Savior Jesus Christ" mean knowing Jesus is still with me at lunch if Greg ruins it? And me not being mean to him if he does? Even though I'll feel like it...*

CRINKLE. A folded piece of paper was pushed into Abigail's hand from behind her in the hall. What was Greg doing now? Trying to give her papercuts? She tried to ignore it. *Help me be nice, God.*

But it happened again, and this time a whisper came too.

"Hey, Chica," Flora's bouncy voice said as quietly as she could. "I had to go to the dentist

this morning, so I didn't get to see you yet, but I made you this. Because you got sick. Did you throw up a lot? Guess what? Birds throw up on purpose to feed their babies! Gross! Are you feeling better?"

Abigail unfolded the paper in her hand, glancing down to see a homemade card.

Flora still wanted to be friends! Just like Mom thought she would.

"Are you feeling better, Chica?" Flora repeated as they sat down in the cafeteria.

"Oh, yeah," Abigail said lightly, even though she felt nervous still.

"Sorry you got sick," Flora said again, nicely.

"Well, it wasn't sick-sick," Abigail tried to explain, worrying that Flora might think she had germs.

Flora took a bite of her sandwich. "What kind of sick was it?" she asked curiously.

"Um, well," Abigail said, remembering how

much better she'd felt the first time they had lunch together when she told Flora all about the paint mess. "I just got so worried and upset about so many things for so many days, my stomach was hurting so bad that... I, well, you know..."

She trailed off, looking at Flora anxiously.

"Guess what?" Flora said. "That happened to me one time too!"

"Really?" Abigail exclaimed.

"Oh yeah," Flora answered through a mouthful of food. "How cooooome... you were... so upsssset?" she added, giggling as she chew-talked.

Giggling back, Abigail said, "Well, it's a crazy story. Are you ready?"

Flora's dark curls bounced as she nodded enthusiastically and took another big bite, eyes fixed on Abigail.

⭐ Chapter Twenty

Not Such a Mess

"Soooo," Abigail began as dramatically as she could, "the other day after school I went to my Nana and Grandpa's. Except..." She leaned in very close like she was telling a secret. "They weren't there! I was all alone!"

"Dun-dun-dun!" Flora exclaimed like she was helping narrate a movie.

Thinking about the last few days was suddenly kind of fun. Abigail got on a roll in her storytelling. She explained about Snickers and the birdseed spill, and about the chaos in her new house, and then...

"And THEN," Abigail said without thinking, "I got to school and I was soooo lonely! Because..."

She paused.

Flora tilted her head, ready for the next dramatic scene in the story.

Abigail stared back wide-eyed. She couldn't say that she'd been lonely because Flora had forgotten about her. What if Flora got mad and didn't want to be friends anymore?

"Why? What happened?" Flora asked, on the edge of her seat.

"Well, umm," Abigail answered, "I lost where I was going. Ummm..."

"Let's see," Flora said thoughtfully. "That would have been... Thursday. When you threw up. But it was before that. What happened at lunch that day before you threw up? I might remember. Guess what? I have a memory like an owl, Mama says. That's a good thing!" Flora cupped her hands around her pretty, dark eyes and gave a little hoot.

But you didn't remember me that day! Abigail protested in her head, still frozen, not knowing what to say.

"You know, I don't think we sat together on Thursday," Flora continued. "Who did you sit with? I was making lots of new friends that day. Have you met Brianna? She was on TV one time! Hmm... I'm trying to picture if I saw you..."

"Oh, I remember," Abigail said in a hurry, hoping to brush past all the bits about Flora forgetting about her. "I sat with Greg."

"Greg?" Flora cried, wrinkling her nose. "Why?"

"Well..." Abigail tried to think of an explanation as she felt her cheeks get hot and red.

"Why didn't you sit with me?" Flora exclaimed. "Was Greg mean to you? I would have stood up for you, just like you did for me!"

"But you didn't," Abigail blurted out before she could stop herself. Remembering how Flora didn't even notice her that day, or even the day before that, still hurt. "It was just," she added, barely above a whisper, "it was like you forgot all about me that day."

"Oh," Flora said, suddenly quiet. She looked like she was inspecting her fingers for a minute as she stared at them, picking a little around her nails.

"It's okay," Abigail tried to say, asking God in her head to help her give grace, "I just felt really lonely that day."

"I'm sorry," Flora said, her big eyes looking back into Abigail's like she meant it with all her heart. "I guess I was just meeting so many kids I didn't notice my Chica wasn't with me.

I should have noticed, I just... well, I get so excited I want to meet everyone and make sure everybody likes me and sometimes I forget about the friends I already have. I'm sorry. I didn't mean to leave you out. We should stick together, huh?"

Nodding as her cheeks started to feel less hot, Abigail said, "Yeah, let's stick together. And it's okay, really. I want everybody to like me too."

"Really?" Flora said softly, her voice full of feeling bad.

"Yeah, really," Abigail said, even finding herself smiling as she said words she knew felt good once you got them out. "I forgive you. And..."

Flora took a deep breath.

"And I'm glad you're really good at making lots of friends," Abigail said, realizing she meant it as she looked around at all the faces she still didn't know. Flora probably knew everyone's name and something cool about them already! Like Brianna, whoever that was.

"Maybe," Flora grinned, "maybe we're like a terrific team! Because I can help both of us make friends, and you are good at *being* friends with people!"

Smiling again, Abigail repeated what she'd thought the other day. "Miss Abigail Chica Brenner," she announced, spreading her arms out like she was declaring it from a stage, "The Very Good Friend!"

Flora giggled.

"And you're Miss Flora Fantastical Flower Flores," Abigail beamed, spreading her arms again, "Friendliest Friend-Finder Forever!"

"Alliteration!" Flora practically shouted, putting her hands up for a double high-five.

"Go team!" Abigail laughed as she clapped her hands against her friend's. *Thank you, God!* she prayed in her head. *Grace is a really good thing, I think!*

"Ooh! Can we make up a secret handshake at the park today?" Flora asked. "You can still come, right? After school?"

"Yes!" Abigail smiled. "I asked my mom last night!"

"Yay!" Flora exclaimed, taking another big bite of her sandwich and being silly again as she asked with a mouthful, "Soooo, what's our adventure go-in-g to beeee?"

Popping open her Amazing Adventure Box,

Abigail grabbed some sticky notes and her multi-pen. Cramming a whole peanut butter cookie in her mouth and silly-saying, "Wellllll, let's make a plaaan!" she clicked the pen for purple and poised it over the paper.

Chapter Twenty-One

Adventuring

Skipping into the park arm in arm, Abigail and Flora scouted for the best spot to start their adventure. Their plan was to find the biggest rock or the tallest tree and make that their home base.

"There!" they both shouted at once, pointing past a field to a tangle of trees and boulders. As they skipped that way, Abigail imagined the grass was all water and the boulders were boats. She told Flora some of the story about Jesus and Peter walking on water so they could pretend to walk on water too.

But Flora interrupted her with a little fake cough. "Incoming, Captain Commander Chica," she whispered.

Abigail looked past Flora in time to see red sneakers and dark hair. Her eyes met the bright blue eyes of... Greg.

"Oh hey," he said. He was all alone. "What are you doing?"

"Umm, well," Abigail hesitated, "we're going on an adventure."

"Cool," Greg said. "You know, I can climb trees fast. And build fires and stuff."

Everyone was silent for a moment as Greg looked at Abigail and Flora with an awkward smile.

"Umm, well," Abigail answered, suddenly feeling her heart pound.

"This is a girls-only adventure," Flora cut in quickly, squeezing Abigail's arm, "so, bye!"

Pulled along by Flora's extra-fast skipping,

Abigail wondered what just happened as they left Greg alone in the open field. When she glanced back, she saw Greg's head hanging and shoulders sagging as he shuffled towards the woods past the boulders alone. He looked... sad. And lonely.

But there wasn't time to think about that.

"Look! Look!" Flora shouted, dropping Abigail's arm and running up to a rock taller than both of them. Right behind it, a huge, thick tree with lots of tangly branches and big green leaves marked the edge of the woods. "It's perfect!"

"We found home-base island," Abigail answered in her best captain-commander-hero voice.

Jumping up and down next to the rock, Flora said, "I" **THUMP** "can't" **THUMP** "reach" **THUMP** "the" **THUMP** "top!" **THUMP.**

"The adventure begins!" Abigail giggled, running around to the back of the rock, where the tree was. The branches were perfect for using as a ladder! Like a tree-fort rock-base super combo! "Let me scout out the best angle so we can get up," she called out.

"O-" **THUMP** "-kay!" **THUMP,** Flora answered, still jumping up with her arms outstretched, just in case the rock had a good hold she could reach somewhere.

Just as Abigail came around the big rock, she heard something besides Flora's jumping and thumping.

WHOOSH!

Leaves flew up from the ground a little way off through the trees.

WHOOSH!

It happened again.

Was somebody else out there? Abigail peered around some tree trunks. Maybe there was going to be a mysterious woods-monster in their adventure. It could be part sea-monster, part tree-dweller!

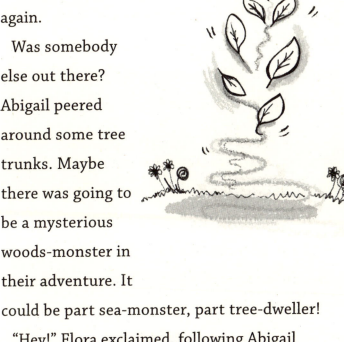

"Hey!" Flora exclaimed, following Abigail around the boulder. "Any luck finding a way up, Chica?"

"Yeah!" Abigail exclaimed, pointing at some big, knotted roots jutting up all around the back of the big rock. "Ready?" she asked, smiling as she clipped her backpack's stomach-strap around her. If you wore that strap in school, you looked silly. On an adventure, though, you looked brave and wise. Abigail swept her hands out like she was announcing a big discovery. "Introducing: our secret entrance to the Big Beautiful Boulder Base!"

Clapping, Flora started to copy her stomach-strap idea to get ready for the climb. "Let's go!"
WHOOSH!

"Arrrgh!" Flora cried, finally jumping up so high she might have actually been able to reach the top of the rock. Her whole face looked like

it jumped too. "What was that?"

"The mystery monster for our adventure," Abigail laughed. "Sorry you were scared... but... your face!"

Laughing too, Flora turned and peeked through the trees. When she looked back at Abigail, her face was much more serious. "It's a monster alright," she whispered. "Greg."

 Chapter Twenty-Two

Second Chances

Abigail pulled herself up a big branch and scrambled the rest of the way over the craggly edges of the rock until she was standing on a nice, flat spot at the top that looked out over the beautiful park. She beamed back down at Flora. "You can see everything from up here! And just look at this lake!" she exclaimed, pretending as she gazed over the grass.

Flora scrambled up next to Abigail. "Big Beautiful Boulder Base: achieved!" she announced, standing up real straight like maybe a cape should be blowing in the wind behind her. "Wow, this is awesome, Chica!"

WHOOSH! WHOOSH!

They could see Greg clearly now, kicking up leaves in the woods. Abigail went quiet, her giggle sinking into guilt. She'd called Greg the monster, but *she'd* been the monster to *him* yesterday.

"Come on, Chica! What kind of mission should we start with?" Flora gave a secret kind of grin. "Let's forget all about that gross, guuhh, geee, bully Greg. I can't think of another G for alliteration!"

Grace! That "g-word" popped right into Abigail's head. But before it could come out of her mouth, another voice butted in.

"Hey, I'm not gross! And not a bully!" Greg's voice carried up to the top of the Boulder Base.

Flora and Abigail both dropped down, surprised and embarrassed. They lay flat on the rock, like maybe, if they stayed low and quiet, everything would be okay.

"I was trying to be funny!" Greg added, with a **WHOOSH! WHOOSH!** as he kicked at leaves even harder.

For a minute, everything went so quiet that Abigail didn't hear the birds in the woods or the shrieks and laughs of kids in the rest of the park. She didn't hear anything but her own breathing, and Flora's, and the thought in her head she just couldn't shake.

I think I know what Jesus would do.

Abigail started crawling on her belly to the edge of the boulder. Flora followed.

"Hey," Greg said again, this time more softly as the four eyes of the two girls appeared over the edge of the boulder and met his. "Look, I'm sorry. I was trying to be funny about your name, and I was trying to have fun doing art together, and I was trying to cheer you up with funny faces today..." He scrunched up his face like he had before, only this time it looked sad. "Look," he said, "I don't have a lot of friends... like you said."

Flora's elbow poked Abigail's side. "What do we do?" she whispered.

"Give us a sec, okay?" Abigail called down to Greg. She and Flora scooted back on their bellies, twisting their heads to look at each other and whisper against the cool, safe surface of the big boulder.

"What do we do about our... monster problem?" Flora whispered.

"Maybe he's not really a monster," Abigail offered. She shrugged. "Maybe we're all a little bit monsters."

Flora wrinkled her nose like she was thinking very hard.

Abigail bit her lip, trying to decide what else Jesus would say. She knew that they were all a little bit monsters because of sin, and that was why everyone needed grace. That was why Jesus came and died, right? And the Bible said to grow in grace and to... Abigail's eyes widened. To give grace!

"Maybe," she suggested to Flora, "we all need second chances. And third and fourth ones."

Flora nodded her head and scrunched her eyebrows seriously, like she'd made a big decision. Suddenly, she scooted forward to the edge again. Abigail followed fast.

"So," Flora announced, "my superpower is making friends." She jerked her head toward Abigail. "My Chica's superpower is *being* friends." Finally, she looked down at Greg. "What are you good at?"

Greg shrugged. "Trying again?" he said dully. "That's what my dad always says about me. I never give up. I just start over and over until I get it right."

Flora looked at Abigail again, not sure what to say.

"I think that sounds like a good superpower," Abigail called down. "We can be the Terrific Team Trio!" Abigail paused. "And... sorry Greg, about, you know, lunch yesterday..."

"It's okay." Greg shrugged again, but he had a smile now.

"Well," Abigail said, "are you coming up?"

Greg answered with **WHOOSH! WHOOSH!** and **THUMP, STOMP** as he ran through the leaves and hurried right up their secret entrance.

Abigail took another deep breath as she felt lots of relief about everything. *Jesus,* she prayed inside excitedly, *I think I just grew in your grace!*

A Note from the Author

Dear reader,

One of my friends has a talent for getting stuck. He's gotten his arm trapped in a vase, his leg caught in a chair, and his whole body tangled up tight in Christmas lights.

Hopefully you don't have that talent too! But I bet you do feel stuck sometimes. Most of us do. Especially in our hearts, when something feels like it's so messed up it can never get better. Especially when we're the ones who messed up!

Thankfully, we're never too stuck to start over.

Of course, we can't go back and change things that have already happened. We don't have time machines (at least, I don't!). But we do have an amazing God.

God is the great unstuckerer.

Just like we see in this story about Abigail, God's grace never runs out. And that means…

1. If we trust in Jesus, we get second, and third, and infinity chances with God because he forgives us.
2. Just because something is messy today, doesn't mean it always will be.
3. God grows us in grace to be like Jesus. He doesn't give up on us when we mess up.

Just as the Bible verse that Abigail learns explains, we get to "grow in the grace and knowledge of our Lord and Savior Jesus Christ" (2 Peter 3:18).

When you feel stuck and when you worry that things can never get better, I hope you'll remember that God's grace never runs out. So not only can *stuff* get better, but as God grows you in grace, *you'll* become better too.

Keep growing in grace!

Your friend,
Bethany

Wish you could join in with Abigail's games? You can! Visit **thegoodbook.com/abigail** to find...

Adventure Central

How to Make an Amazing Adventure Box

Worksheets from Abigail's Kids' Club

Abigail's Animals Game

Sticky-Note Storytelling Tips

Amazing Alliteration Race

Bible-Verse Doodle Printouts

... and more!

Now read on for a sneak peek at Abigail's next adventure!

Abigail rushed off the bus and through the front door, yelling "Hi!" to Mom as she raced to her room. She realized she should make Pedro a cape as inspiration for Panda-gail! And make a cape for herself for Career Day!

Turning into her brightly decorated room, Abigail looked on her bed for Pedro. That was right where she left him, she was sure of it... But where was he?

She looked next to her bed, in case he'd fallen off. No Pedro.

Down on her knees, she looked under her bed and under her desk. Still no Pedro. How far could a stuffed panda with super-snap arms go on his own?

But maybe that was the key. Abigail didn't have to think too hard to solve the mystery. Pedro didn't go anywhere on his own; he was a toy. But Henry was always begging to play with Pedro.

HMMM.

"Henry!" Abigail said in her most grown-up voice, marching off to find him.

"He's out back in the yard!" Mom called from the kitchen. "Wipe your feet when you come back in! I just cleaned the carpets!"

Abigail grabbed her favorite sneakers and shoved them on her feet as fast as she could. She sensed a crime had happened.

She turned the handle and shoved the door open, ready to stop the criminal!

She rushed into the yard...

And there was Henry.

And there was Pedro.

And neither of them were the right colors.

"I caught you panda-handed!" Abigail yelled, slamming the door shut behind her as she marched down the steps toward her muddy brother and poor, slimy panda.

"Gabigaaa..." Henry said in a grumpy voice, like he was ready to fight. It was almost a growl.

"Henry, Pedro is MY panda, not yours!" she said, sticking her hands on her hips like Mom did when someone was in big trouble.

Henry hugged the now-brown and gooey Pedro tighter.

"Mine!" Henry exclaimed.

"No! Mine!" Abigail said, leaping forward and grabbing Pedro's arm to try to set him free.

They tugged back and forth until Abigail lost her grip on Pedro's arm and it snapped— hard—around Henry's.

Like Pedro was trying to hold on.

Time for a different tactic, Abigail thought, frowning. "Henry Abraham," she said sternly, using his whole name just like Dad and Mom did when he was in trouble, "you broke the rules. You stole."

Henry's eyes darted to the back door, and

his knees started to bend like he was going to make a break for it. He was going to run into the house! And get mud everywhere! On Mom's clean carpets!

PHWEEE! PHWEEE!

Abigail swiftly pulled her whistle and shiny badge out of her pocket and blew the whistle very loudly. She pointed her badge at Henry and whistled and whistled. He jumped, surprised, and screeched with wide, scared eyes, "No wee-sill, no wee-sill!"

SPLASH.

A little bit of mud splattered onto Abigail's purple-glitter sneakers.

That was it. Abigail was ready to lose it...

Find out what happens next in:

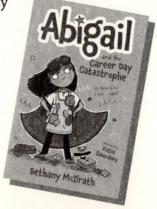

Book-Club Questions

For Chapters 1-3

1. Have you ever felt nervous and excited at the same time? Why did you feel both ways at once?
2. Abigail remembers a story about Simon Peter and Jesus from Luke 5:1-5. Look up this story. Can you tell what Simon Peter thinks about Jesus? What do you think Abigail thinks about Jesus?
3. Do you think most people worry about what other people will think about them? What do you think most people want others to think about them?

For Chapters 4-5

4. If you were going to make an Adventure Central, what would it be like?

5. Why is Abigail so disappointed about her Adventure Central? Have you ever felt that way? What did you do?

6. What would you do if you were unfairly blamed for something? What if you tried to explain but nobody listened?

For Chapters 6-8

7. How did you become friends with the people you are closest to? What kinds of things change in your heart or life when you make a friend?

8. Look up Micah 6:8 in the Bible. How did Abigail do what this verse says when she stood up for Flora?

9. If someone you care about is upset, what do you do to cheer them up? How do you feel when you cheer someone else up?

For Chapters 9-11

10. If you were in Abigail's kids' club, what fun fact would you share about yourself?
11. What does grace mean? Are there any other Bible words that you kind of know about, but you're not really sure what they mean?
12. Look up Luke 5:1-11 in the Bible. Why do you think Simon Peter told Jesus he was a sinner? What did Jesus say back to Simon Peter?

For Chapters 12-14

13. How would you feel if you were locked outside alone like Abigail? What would you do if you were in her situation?
14. What makes something an accident, and what makes it your fault? What advice would you give Abigail about the birdseed spill and Snickers?
15. Look up Matthew 14:22-33 in the Bible (or find it in chapter 14 of this book). Why do you

think Jesus helped Peter in this story? Why did Peter need help?

Chapters 15-18

16. How do you think Abigail was feeling about Flora in the cafeteria? What was she feeling about Greg?

17. Look up John 21:15-17 in the Bible (or find it in chapter 18 of this book). How do we know that Jesus has forgiven Simon Peter? How can Jesus forgive him even though Simon Peter has messed up so much?

18. What makes asking God for forgiveness so good? How does it feel when God gives you grace?

Chapters 19-22

19. If you were Abigail, how would you feel about giving grace to Flora, and about telling her she hurt your feelings?

20. Do you think Abigail's right that we're "all a little bit monsters"? Why?
21. Can you think of ways God has given you grace? And that other people have given you grace? How about ways you can show grace to others?

Acknowledgments

I'm still surprised I have had the privilege of writing this book. Thank you, dear Jesus, for the honor and delight of getting to participate in this particular good work in you, and for the grace you so freely and gently give me daily.

Thank you to the people who somehow are not surprised that this book has come to be and have urged me on all along.

To Matt, who has been faithfully praying for Abigail's future friends since this idea began, who loved her (and me) through many growing pains, and whose qualities show up in some of the best traits and conversations on these pages. I'm so grateful God gave me you to follow him beside.

So many others have read, prayed, listened to my ramblings, and encouraged me in this adventure. I thank God for each of you! To name a few: Mumsy and Mr, Dan and Miriam, Matty, Cilla, Shannon, Jane, Pam, Joanne, Abby, Lois, Lesley, Heather, Abbey, Bob and Lauren, Jaci and Elijah, Piper, the Strahms, the Tolstiks, and our New City family.

Thank you also to those who helped shape the story as beta-readers, especially the earliest readers —Nora, Rani, Evie, Isabel, Jess, Jemima, Emma, and Rachel. Thank you to many others whose quips, questions, and quandaries over the years have helped me know just what Abigail needed. I wish I could mention everyone!

A big thank you to Katie Saunders, who has made Abigail's inner life and real world so vivid through her brilliant illustrations.

Lastly, thank you to my brothers and sisters in Christ at The Good Book Company for the joy of serving alongside you in this way. Thank you especially to Katy, whose watchful, playful eye has kept Abigail in just the right amount of trouble, and to "Aunt" Abigail, who so constantly shares in the serendipity of this story with me and has created an Adventure Central for all to enjoy.

BIBLICAL | RELEVANT | ACCESSIBLE

At The Good Book Company, we are dedicated to helping Christians and local churches grow. We believe that God's growth process always starts with hearing clearly what he has said to us through his timeless word—the Bible.

Ever since we opened our doors in 1991, we have been striving to produce Bible-based resources that bring glory to God. We have grown to become an international provider of user-friendly resources to the Christian community, with believers of all backgrounds and denominations using our books, Bible studies, devotionals, evangelistic resources, and DVD-based courses.

We want to equip ordinary Christians to live for Christ day by day, and churches to grow in their knowledge of God, their love for one another, and the effectiveness of their outreach.

Call us for a discussion of your needs or visit one of our local websites for more information on the resources and services we provide.

Your friends at The Good Book Company

thegoodbook.com | thegoodbook.co.uk
thegoodbook.com.au | thegoodbook.co.nz
thegoodbook.co.in